'Nothing comes close to you. The way you soothe
everything inside of me right down to my soul when
I'm with you. I'm not willing to ever give that up.'
~Seth~

To all the foolish, reckless, risk takers.
You are irreplaceable.

One Penny

A

Marked Heart

Novel

M. Sembera

One Penny
Copyright 2015 © M. Sembera
ISBN: 978-0692337875
Edited by Margaret Civella
Cover Design Copyright 2014 © M. Sembera
Manifeesto, Zurijeta_/Shutterstock
Published by
Broken Bird Media

For more information contact:
M.Sembera@brokenbirdmedia.com
One Penny is a work of fiction. All names, Characters, places and incidents are the product of the author's imagination.

Place name and any resemblance to events or actual persons, living or dead, are entirely coincidental.

Celtic Heart vector art featured with quote provided Oleg Zhevelev/Shutterstock

The Wren and Celtic Heart logo is an original piece of art created specifically for M. Sembera.

Table of Contents

Foolish is the heart that leaves itself open to falling in love. Reckless is the person who steps away from tradition to claim a life of their own. Irreplaceable is the moment one takes the risk.

One

Enjoying the sound of the raindrops as they bounced off of her umbrella and fell around her, Penny couldn't have been happier. Her brother Auggie had proposed to her roommate and good friend, Charlotte, and Charlotte said yes. Penny loved her job at Legacy Ink, although she still hid working there from most of her family. Not to mention, for six months she had been dating Brooks, the drummer in her brother Braden's band. That was a personal record for her and the fact that he'd hung around for more than a week or two, led Penny to believe he just might be the one.

After spotting Brooks' car in the parking lot, Penny skipped up the steps to her second floor apartment. She couldn't wait to get inside and see her boyfriend. Thinking maybe all the wedding talk had inspired him, Brooks never just stopped by without calling first. Excited and hopeful, Penny closed her umbrella, gave it a little shake and propped it up against the wall before heading inside.

Stepping into her apartment, she glanced around before heading to her room. Wondering if she would find flowers or rose petals covering the bed or even better strawberries and chocolate. All Penny saw when she walked into her room was Brooks standing there, surprised to see her.

"I thought you wouldn't be home until later," he said, appearing unsure of himself.

Thinking, 'he's nervous, nervous is good' Penny replied, "Kieran didn't have anymore appointments today so he closed up early."

Reaching up to scratch the back of his head, Brooks informed, "I was really hoping to do this before you got home."

A slight scowl formed as she thought 'Okay, now he is just being weird'.

"Do what?" she asked, now noticing a box on the floor by her bed.

Tilting his head to the side, Brooks answered, "Ah Penny, I like you, a lot, and you're so much fun to be around..."

She knew what was coming next as she said, "Oh, Okay."

"Thing is, I don't want anything serious right now. Ya know?"

Nodding Penny thought 'this is the ninth time I've heard that', as she repeated, "Yea, okay."

"It's just too much pressure. I'm always worried that I'll do something wrong and your brothers will take it personal."

"Okay," Penny repeated for a third time, thinking it wasn't necessary to point out every little thing that made him not want to be with her.

"And yesterday I had to lie to your mom because you were at the shop..."

"I get it, alright," she griped, feeling more frustrated with him than anything else at this point.

"Still friends?" he asked with a smile.

Watching him pick his box up and start to leave she replied, "Sure."

As he headed out of her room, Brooks turned to her, asking, "Oh, can you tell your brothers it was a mutual break up? I don't want to get my ass beat over this."

"Yea, sure."

"Thanks Penny. You're the best," he assured as he continued out of her room and then her apartment.

Standing in her bedroom, after another failed relationship, Penny thought 'That's it, I give up'.

⌘

Sitting on her couch between her roommate Charlotte and her cousin Kieran's wife Liv, Penny dipped her finger in the peanut butter jar before smoothing it over her Hershey bar and taking a bite.

Cringing as she watched Penny, Charlotte asked, "So let me get this straight. He wasn't even going to break up with you in person and you're still going to cover his butt, so Auggie doesn't get mad?"

Shrugging a shoulder at Charlotte, Penny replied, "It's not that big of a deal and besides, I don't want to be with anyone who doesn't want to be with me. So, it might as well have been mutual."

"Mutual my ass," Liv blurted before saying, "Showing up with a box while you're not home is not mutual. It's a jerk move."

"There were only two t-shirts and a tooth brush in the box," Penny replied as she made a face at Charlotte for reaching over and grabbing the jar of peanut butter out of her hand.

Making her way to the kitchen, Charlotte fussed, "Sticking your nasty fingers in the peanut butter isn't going to solve anything."

Pursing her lips into a smile, Penny shouted after Charlotte, "My fingers aren't nasty they're delicious."

Laughing at the two of them, Liv shook her head before announcing, "Alright Delicious Fingers, I gotta go."

As Charlotte shouted, "Bye," from the kitchen, Penny said, "You're gonna tell Kieran aren't you?"

"I sure am, but he won't say anything."

Frowning, Penny asked, "What do you think I did wrong?"

"Nothing at all beautiful, but next time, be more selective about who you get down with. Sex should be a bonus to being with you not the reason a guy is with you. Ya know?"

Nodding, Penny hugged her.

13

Standing up, Liv shared, "And that's coming from someone whose first time was in a friend's passenger seat with a cute drunk guy who got into the wrong car."

Penny laughed as Liv made a clicking sound with her mouth, winked and heading out of the apartment.

Sweeping her long auburn hair over her shoulder, Penny sunk back onto the couch. Holding onto the bottom of her hair, she brushed her fingers across the ends thinking about what Liv said.

⌘

Standing at the bottom of the steps that led to his new apartment, Seth was one more call sent to voice mail away from banging his head against the railing. What kind of place doesn't have after hour's maintenance? Willing maintenance to answer his call, he heard someone clear their throat from behind him.

Turning he looked up the stairs and saw a woman wearing a hot pink tank top with black slack and black and white tennis shoes. She had long black hair that was pinned up at the sides and colorful full sleeve tattoos.

Tapping her foot, she griped, "Am I interrupting you?"

Seth pulled his phone from his ear, saying, "I'm sorry. No, I was... I didn't know anyone was trying to come down the stairs."

With an over exaggerated nod, she fussed, "Could ya move out of the way?"

"Sorry," he repeated as he stepped to the side before asking, "Hey, do you live here?"

Passing him by, she replied, "Nope, just visitin'."

Seth looked down at his phone and dialed again.

"Great," he mumbled.

"Do you?"

Glancing up from his cell phone, Seth replied, "Do I what?"

"Do you live here or are you a lurker? Tryin' to pick up woman."

Instantly defensive, he said, "I'm not lurking, I'm trying to move in. I had all the utilities turned on last week but there's still no power. The electric company swears it's not on their end. It was raining so I had to wait to start moving and now the manager's office is closed and I can't get ahold of anyone."

After letting out a loud, "Ha!" she clapped her hands together, saying, "You're having some kinda bad day."
Shaking his head as he slid his phone into his back pocket, he couldn't help but laugh at all of his bad luck.

"I'm Liv, just so ya know and my girls upstairs might be able to help."

"What apartment?"

"317, it's the one with the umbrella beside the door."

Thinking there might be a bright side to this day after all, he replied, "Thank you so much. And I'm Seth."
Liv started to turn around then stopped.

"Word to the wise, Seth, the blonde one's taken and the red head, she's nothin' but trouble," Liv advised before snapping her fingers and then pointing at him.
Nodding at her it was hard to tell if she was serious. Shaking off his encounter with the most interesting woman he'd probably ever met, Seth turned and headed up the stairs.

⌘

Sulking on the couch, Penny sighed when she heard a knock at the door.

"Auggie's here," she shouted to Charlotte, who was in her room getting ready to go to work.

"No he's not, I'm driving tonight," she hollered back.
Dragging herself off of the couch, she made her way to the door.

Penny smiled up at the tall, handsome, brown-haired man with a startled look on his face. As she looked him

15

over there was something familiar about him. Then, she realized, she knew him.

"Seth?"

"No," he uttered shaking his head before rambling, "I mean yes... Never mind... Sorry," and then turned away. Watching as he bumped into the railing on his way down the stairs, Penny waited to shut the door until she saw him sprinting across the parking lot. It seemed like he couldn't get away from her fast enough.

"Who was at the door?"

With a confused expression, Penny replied, "A guy I went to high school with."

Shaking her head, Charlotte laughed, "They really do start lining up at your door don't they."

Penny couldn't help but laugh at the thought.

"So what did he want?"

"No idea, he just said never mind and then ran away."

⌘

Sitting in the cab of the moving truck he'd rented, Seth could feel an anxiety attack coming on. No wonder everything was going wrong today. It had to be a bad omen. Gripping the steering wheel as tight as he could, Seth closed his eyes. Concentrating on his breathing, he inhaled through his nose and slowly exhaled out from his mouth trying to create the calming rhythm years of therapy had taught him.

Once he had relaxed enough to think rationally, Seth decided to wait the night out in the moving truck and first thing in the morning when the apartment manager's office opened he would request a different apartment. There was no way he would be able to live right next door to Penny Caffrey. He wouldn't survive it.

Two

Trying his hardest to make the apartment manager Marty, understand how important switching apartments was without explaining the reason why seemed easier in Seth's head. Once she'd explained that the lack of electricity to his apartment was nothing more than a simple flip of a breaker switch, the forty something apartment manager with short brown frizzy hair and red-rimmed eyeglasses seemed put out with everything else he had to say.

Anxiety filled him as the realization that he was stuck, grew more apparent with each moment Marty stared back at him with her unwavering disposition.

Breaking the silence with an unapologetic sigh, she assured, "There is nothing I can do."

"You're telling me there are no other apartments available?"

"The best I can do is put you back on the waiting list until another apartment becomes available."

"What am I supposed to do until then?" Seth questioned.

"Move into the apartment you already have," she replied in a snarky sort of way.

Ready to make one last plea for a different apartment, Seth noticed Marty's expression change.

Completely ignoring him now, Marty gave a cheerful wave towards the door and walked from behind the desk and into a back room. When Seth turned to see who had walked in, he could feel his knees start to buckle.

Shrugging her shoulders up as she smiled, Penny gave a soft, "Hi," the moment he looked at her.

He watched her expression change from a pleasant smile to a disappointed pout when he gave her a quick nod in response.

"Here you go," Marty said startling them both.

Penny's smile quickly returned as she took a package from her saying, "Thanks! I think this is the last one."

"No problem hun," Marty replied before glaring at Seth questioning, "Was there anything else I can help you with?" Seth couldn't help the ridiculous look he gave her. She hadn't helped him out at all.

⌘

The second Penny made it back to her apartment, she swung the door closed, quickly set her package down and stared out of the peephole. From her balcony she could clearly see the front of the Manager's office and the view from the peephole in her door was just as good. She watched Seth walk out of the office and over to a Uhaul truck before placing his hands against the side of it as he seemed to bang his head into the truck.

"Whatcha doin'?"

Penny jumped a little before glancing back at Charlotte as she answered, "Shh, I'm spying on him."

Charlotte laughed, asking, "Who?"

"That guy I went to high school with," Penny replied, returning her eye to the peephole.

Quickly at her side, Charlotte said, "The guy from yesterday? Let me see."

Penny moved to the side.

"I don't see anyone."

"He was just there by the Uhaul truck," she swore as Charlotte moved away from the door.

Scanning the parking lot, Charlotte was right, he wasn't there anymore.

Sighing, Penny leaned her back against the door.

"So what's the deal with this guy?" Charlotte questioned before saying, "Yesterday he knocks on our door and now he's hanging out in the parking lot. Oh, I bet he's moving in! Maybe he's got the apartment next door."

"Great," Penny mumbled.

"You don't like him?"

Shrugging a shoulder at Charlotte, Penny shared, "I don't think he likes me."

"That's impossible. You're Penny. Everyone loves you."

"I know, Right!" Penny agreed as she stepped away from the door.

"So? What's the story?"

With a little sigh, she replied, "We went out once in high school."

"And?"

"Well, Remember how I told you when my first real date came to pick me up from the house, Auggie and Braden took him to the back yard, showed him our little pet cemetery and told him that all the other boys I'd gone out with were buried there?"

Clearly amused, Charlotte replied, "And he was so scared he wouldn't sit next to you at the movies."

Nodding, Penny pointed to the door, saying, "That's him."

Practically lunging at the door, Charlotte blurted, "Oh, I have got to see this guy."

Giving a little laugh, Penny grabbed her package and took it to her room.

Charlotte was still standing at the door staring out of the peephole when Penny walked back into the room.

"Someone's coming up the stairs!" she announced.

Penny made her way over to Charlotte as she moved out of the way allowing Penny to take a look.

Seeing Seth carrying a box Penny said, "Yep, guess he's our new neighbor," before stepping away from the door.

Charlotte peered out of the peephole again, then looked back at Penny with a confused expression.

"That's Seth."

Equally confused, Penny replied, "I know that's Seth. How do you know that's Seth?"

"He works for Jackson at JPT Financial," Charlotte informed before sharing, "I met him right after I started managing the bar. He's Jackson's personal assistant or something like that."

Holding her hands up, Penny shook her head, saying, "Wait... That's Secretary Seth?" trying to make sense of this knew found information.

Charlotte stared at her saying, "Seth is Boyfriend Graveyard?"

Both Penny and Charlotte burst into laughter.

⌘

Sitting down on the floor of his new apartment, Seth stared at his cell phone. Seven missed calls since eight o'clock last night. All from his father. He purposely let the calls go to voice mail instead of being forced to lie. He couldn't tell him he spent the night, cramped in the cab of the Uhaul truck. Especially since the whole point of moving to Golden Glen, the most exclusive apartment complex in the area, was to show his father he was successful in his chosen occupation. Most people would have been proud of someone who worked full-time and went to school. Accounting was a good profession. All his family cared about though, was that he wasn't a doctor like his grandfather, father and uncles. When he broke the news right after he graduated, his mother Linda stayed in bed for two weeks crying because she said he broke her heart. His own grandmother even called him a disappointment but his father was the worst. Seth's father Leonard was domineering, overbearing and not one to mince words. It took him all of two seconds to let Seth know how worthless he was as a son.

Feeling a tension headache coming on, Seth set his phone on his lap and rubbed his temples. Telling himself that he was a twenty seven year-old grown man. A man with a career that he'd worked hard for all on his own. But it didn't stop the surge of pain to his brain and instant stomach cramps the second his cell phone rang.

Before Seth could say 'hello' his father stated, "Nice you finally decided to answer."

"I..." was all Seth could get out before Leonard informed, "Your mother and I will be there at noon to see your apartment."

Seth started to say 'Yes Sir' but the call disconnected before he had the chance.

⌘

Curled up in her comforter on the couch, Penny had spent the majority of her day spying on Seth out of her peephole. At one point he had two guys helping him move furniture up the stairs but they left right after they finished. Aside from that it was just him carrying boxes up to his apartment. In a way, she kind of felt bad he was moving practically all by himself but then again she couldn't really remember him having a lot of friends either.

What Penny remembered of Seth from high school was that he was shy and mostly kept to himself. He actually took an F in English class instead of reading his essay in front of the class. She was really surprised when he asked her out on a date. He'd never even spoken to her before then. When she said 'yes' all he said was 'okay, great' and didn't say another word to her until he came to pick her up. After Auggie and Braden scared the crap out of him, he hardly spoke to her. When he dropped her off two hours before she had to be home, he walked her to the door then quickly back to his and left. He never spoke to her after that.

She had always thought Seth was cute. A tad on the dorky side but that made him even more adorable. He had grown up very handsome. Too bad he was still so shy or just didn't like her. It was just as well since Penny had decided to swear off men for a while. Still they were neighbors and it would be nice to at least say hello.

Three

As spacious as his new apartment was, with his parents nitpicking every inch of it, Seth felt like it was too small for the three of them. He'd already gotten sick twice waiting for them to arrive and now that it felt like the walls were closing in on him, he needed to get some air.

Stepping out onto his balcony, Seth tensed when the apartment door next to his opened. There was a sense of relief when a beautiful blonde walked out instead of Penny. It was Charlotte, manager of The Dog House bar that his boss Jackson Thomas owned. She had to have been the one that Liv said was taken. Seth realized this as he made the connection between her and Penny. Of course they were roommates. She was engaged to Penny's oldest brother Auggie.

Seth watched Charlotte close the door behind her before she glanced over at him.

"Small world," he greeted.

Charlotte replied, "Sure is," before asking "How do you like it here so far?"

Seth smiled as he said, "I just moved in yesterday."

Nodding she started to say, "So a..." when Seth's parents walked out.

As he started to make introductions, his mother blurted, "Charlotte Roberts."

Giving a polite smile, Charlotte greeted, "Mrs. Chevalier."

Seth watched as his mother placed one hand on her chest and the other against his father's arm informing, "She's Society," before assuring Charlotte, "Please, it's Linda."

Her smile was a bit forced now as she replied, "Actually, my sister Silvia holds a seat. I opted out."

Seth watched his mother quickly mask a frown as his father asked, "You are Emerson and Amila's daughter?"

Charlotte gave a quick nod before Linda shared, "Your wedding is going to be the event of the season."

"Thank you," Charlotte replied before saying, "I believe the invitations will go out soon."

"I received your 'Save the Date'. I'm not sure I know your fiancé. Is he a business owner?"

The corner of Charlotte's mouth curled up into a smile as she answered, "No, he's a bartender."

Seth could see the displeasure on his mother's face as she questioned, "Oh, does he live here with you?"

"No, he owns his own home," she replied in a short tone.

Suddenly nudged forward by his father, Seth gave an apologetic smile to Charlotte as Leonard stated, "A young woman needs someone to look out for her in a place like this. Your father should not have allowed you to move here alone."

Charlotte appeared as though she was going to lose it when suddenly, Liv appeared at the top of the stairs.

Wearing black and white plaid slacks with a white tank top and tennis shoes this time, Liv stopped to look everyone over before focusing on Seth.

Snapping her fingers, she pointed at him, saying, "Lurker, hope your day got better."

Seth closed his eyes for a moment and shook his head trying not to laugh.

"Penny inside?" she asked.

"In the kitchen, Liv."

Already knowing his parents disapproved of someone like Liv, they didn't acknowledge her at all before or after she stepped into the apartment.

Linda quickly questioned, "Penny?"

"My roommate," Charlotte snapped glaring at Seth's father.

"Would I know her?"

Charlotte looked directly at Seth as she replied, "I doubt it. Penny is Augustus' sister."

Seth could feel himself tense at the mere mention of her name.

"That's so sweet of you to let her live with you."

Giving his mother a dirty look, Charlotte replied, "Yea, especially since she pays half the rent."

"What is her profession?" Leonard questioned.

"She works for Liv's husband at Legacy Ink," Charlotte answered.

"Is that a print company of sorts?" he inquired.

Standing up tall she stated, "No, it's a tattoo shop."

Charlotte gave a sarcastic smile as if she was just waiting for his parents to make a comment.

The balcony was silent for a moment before Leonard stated, "Give your father my best," as he pushed past his wife and made his way down the stairs.

Glaring at Linda, Charlotte replied, "Oh, I'll be sure to tell Emerson."

Her reply seemed more like a threat than anything else and Seth watched his mother give Charlotte a weak smile before following after his father.

Charlotte's family was pretty infamous. Her grandfather basically owned the town before he died and although her father Emerson chose a different route in life, the name Roberts still carried just as much weight.

With his parents gone, Seth felt like he could breathe again.

Leaning against the balcony, he looked at Charlotte saying, "Sorry about that."

"Eh, don't worry about it. I'm used to dealing with snotty people."

Seth laughed, asking, "How long have you lived here?"

"It's getting close to a year now," she replied before sharing, "After the wedding, it'll just be Penny here."
Nodding at her, Seth could tell she knew something.

Rolling her eyes at him she smiled, offering, "If you get bored or want some company, your welcome anytime. I'm not here a lot lately, but Penny is."
Seth nodded at her again as she turned and headed down the stairs.

⌘

It was hard for Penny to understand why Seth would talk to Charlotte and Liv but not her. She never personally did anything to him. Not to mention how ridiculous it would be if he was holding something her brothers did ten years ago against her. They were just being big brothers and seriously, how could he have believed them.

Liv appeared sympathetic as she said, "Sometimes things like that just stick with a person."

"One of the crosses said RIP Mr. Flufferton."

"Hey, you could have had a thing for hairy British guys."
Penny laughed almost spilling her little pot of beeswax on the kitchen counter.

"What can I say Pen, boys are dumb and they get even dumber when they really like a girl."

Agreeing with her, Penny nodded asking, "Speaking of dumbass boys. How's Braden?"

"Same. He shows up every Thursday at the house for beer and pizza but doesn't say much." Penny could tell Liv was upset over Braden behavior lately as she quickly changed the subject, asking, "What flavor are you doing this time?"

Pulling her hair up into a knot on the top of her head, Penny walked to the kitchen table that was covered in little slide tins where Liv was sitting and replied, "Fair's coming up. So, cotton candy."

"Yummy, I love it!" Liv blurted.

Feeling excited too, Penny said, "I'm making a few batches, how many do you want?"

"All of them," she laughed before saying, "But since I'm not the only one obsessed with your homemade lip balms, I'll try not to be stingy and take five."

Penny giggled as she shared, "I'll bring yours to the shop tomorrow."

Liv kicked her feet up on the chair in front of her as she watched Penny fill the tiny slide tins.

Once Penny was finished she left the lip balms on the table to set up while she and Liv sat on the couch in the living room.

Penny was back to dwelling on her new neighbor when Liv interrupted her thoughts by asking, "When are you going to bite the bullet and let Kieran tattoo you?"

Grabbing one of the throw pillows off of the couch, Penny set it on her lap and then leaned forward and buried her face in it.

Liv tapped her on the shoulder assuring, "Kieran's not going to change his mind."

Springing back up she blurted, "He might!"

"How long have you known your cousin?"

"Ugh, why do I have to get one to learn how?"

Liv cocked her head to the side as she insisted, "No self-respecting client is going to let some girl that doesn't even have a tattoo herself, go to work on them."

"Can't I just pretend to have them and say they're hidden?"

"You could, but Kieran will know you don't and won't teach you."

Penny felt ashamed of herself as she admitted, "I'm scared though."

"There's nothing to be afraid of."

"Well, that's easy for you to say, you have a million of them."

"Ha!" Liv blurted before correcting, "Thirty-five, thank you very much and I started with just one."

"Which one?"

Liv gave a soft smile but it seemed more to herself than at Penny as she pointed to the guitar on the inside of her upper arm.

"Does it stand for anything?"

Penny noticed a far off look in Liv's eyes before she gave a loud laugh answering, "Yeah! Being young and stupid."

"If your first one was because you were dumb, why are you advising me to get one?"

With a heavy sigh, she griped, "The tattoo symbolizes when I had my head so far up my ass over a boy, I couldn't think straight. But this isn't about me Pen, it's about you. You wanna station at Kieran's shop? Then stop being scared."

Penny shrunk back a little saying, "Geez, alright."

Reaching over Liv hugged her before standing up as she said, "You can't go around being afraid of what you really want." Penny looked up at her as she continued, "When you have the opportunity, take it. It's no guarantee things will work out the way you want, but you never know until take that step."

Nodding at her, Penny knew she was right. At the same time, it felt like Liv was talking about more than just getting a tattoo.

When Liv left, Penny sat on the couch thinking. She had been in a rut for a while. Without realizing it, all the days that had passed along with various guys she dated had turned into years of the exact same thing. She still needed to work up the courage to get a tattoo but there were other things she could do and she was going to start first thing tomorrow morning. Tomorrow Penny was going to wake up and do things differently and it was going to be awesome.

Four

Bending over the kitchen counter Penny inhaled the delightful scent of her freshly baked cherry pecan muffin as the butter melted on top of it. The smell was just as invigorating as the four cups of coffee she'd already had since she woke at five this morning. As the oven timer echoed throughout the kitchen, she took a quick bite before slipping her hands into a set of oven mitts.

After pulling out her second batch of muffins and setting them on the cooling rack, Penny looked up to see Charlotte standing in the kitchen scowling at her.

"What on earth are you doing?" she questioned, clearly still half asleep.

"Baking muffins!" Penny cheered before offering, "Want some?"

"It is six-thirty in the morning..."

"So, you don't want any muffins?"

Charlotte let out a slight huff before saying, "Well, I'm up now."

Smiling wide, Penny grabbed a plate and set two muffins on it before handing it to Charlotte.

Penny waited for Charlotte to finish her muffins before deciding to let her in on her plans.

"Would you like to know why I'm in such a good mood?"

"You're always in a good mood."

Trying again, Penny asked, "Would you like to know why I'm extra happy today?"

Smiling, Charlotte replied, "Sure."

"I've decided not to have sex anymore."

Practically choking on her cup of coffee, Charlotte questioned, "And that makes you happy?"

"Well, no, but I'm happy with my decision."

"And now you're going to dedicate your life to baking muffins?" Charlotte teased.

Rolling her eyes, Penny laughed, "The muffins are for our new neighbor."

Charlotte started to nod then snapped, "Wait! What?"

"I'm going to make friends with him."

Narrowing her eyes at Penny, Charlotte said, "I thought you were giving up sex..."

"Oh, I am. I've never been friends with a guy before we had sex so I thought Seth moving in next door will be the perfect opportunity to try it out."

"You want to make friends with someone who won't speak to you and practically runs away every time he sees you?"

"Unhunh," Penny replied, taking four muffins, setting them on a plate and walking towards the front door.

As Penny set the plate of muffins on the little table next to the door, Charlotte asked, "What are you doing?"

"I'm going to watch for him to come out so I can give him his muffins."

There was a hint of sarcasm in Charlotte's voice as she warned, "You know, there's a fine line between friendly and stalker."

Penny shot her an absurd look before staring out of the peephole.

⌘

Of course Seth was running late for work, it had been one disaster after another since Friday afternoon. Now here it is, Monday morning he was late for work because his phone died in the middle of the night. Then to make matters worse, he had to change his suit after spilling coffee all over himself in a rush to get ready. Finally, he grabbed his briefcase and hurried out the door.

The moment he stepped onto the balcony, he froze. Penny was standing right in front of him with a plate of muffins in her hand.

"Good Morning!" she cheered, blocking his only exit.

Seth stared at her wondering why she was standing there.

Holding the plate out to him, she informed, "I baked you some muffins."

Shaking his head at her, Seth thought 'who does that?' as he waited for her to get the hint and move out of the way.

Persistent with the muffins she shared, "They're cherry pecan."

"I... a... I'm running late," he finally forced out.

Pursing her lips into a smile, she assured, "No problem, you can take them to go," as she revealed a small paper sack from under the plate.

Seth watched her place the muffins in the paper sack thinking 'she is crazy'.

He carefully took the bag from her as she encouraged, "Have a nice day."

The second she stepped to the side he raced down the stairs.

Making it to his car he quickly hopped in and locked the doors. Taking a moment to catch his breath before he started the engine, he set his briefcase in the passenger seat and set the bag of muffins on top of it. He was starving and they smelled great but there was no way he was going to eat Crazy Penny Muffins. Because seriously, who does that?

⌘

Skipping into Legacy Ink, Penny felt good about how her morning went. It may not have been great but it was a start, and went better than she had expected.

Kieran stepped out of the back. Giving Penny a head nod, he continued to his station in the corner of the shop. Penny watched him as he turned on the lamp and sat down to work on the back piece design he was trying to finish.

Liv walked in from the back marched over to him and she stopped in front of him with her arms crossed.

"Conversation's over Liv," he stated without looking up at her.

"Why? Because you say so?" she snapped at him.

Kieran set his pencil down and looked up at her answering, "Yes."

"Oh! Hell! No!"

Kieran picked his pencil back up, looked down at his drawing and said, "Get outta my shop Liv."

Without being able to help it, Penny gasped. She couldn't believe he said that to her.

"Screw you and your shop," Liv blurted before storming off to the back.

Penny heard the back door slam shut.

Kieran placed his forehead in his hands, closed his eyes and shook his head.

"That was mean," Penny griped.

Without looking up, he asked, "You wanna get out too?"

Shrugging her shoulder at him, she asked, "Do I still get paid?"

Wheeling his chair back, he gave a laugh while shaking his head.

"She wants to have a kid."

Penny's eyes lit up as she cheered, "Really?"

Standing up, Kieran walked to the other side of the room, "I said no."

Instantly disappointed, Penny asked, "Why?"

"Because, one minute she's talking about babies and in the next getting her nipples pierced."

Pressing her wrists against her chest, she muttered, "Ouch," before saying, "So?"

Shaking his head at himself, he replied, "That's not why..."

Penny walked behind the counter, set her elbows down and rested her chin in her palms asking, "What's wrong with you?"

Crossing his arms against his chest, Kieran shared, "I been thinkin' a lot about my legacy."

"Wouldn't it make sense to have a kid then?"

Without answering her, he asked, "You think I was wrong for marking Braden?"

"Yea, I do."

Nodding, Kieran's jaw tightened as he shared, "Every man in our family that's had their heart marked. They found the one, had their heart drawn out, and got the mark. All of 'em stayed together." Rubbing his hand against the Celtic heart tattooed on the left side of his chest with Liv written above it, he continued, "Every damn one."

Seeing the distress in his eyes, Penny tried to make him feel better saying, "Well maybe Braden's was cursed to begin with because your drawer used one she already had instead of making a new one."

"I can't blame your mom for something I did."

"I wish you hadn't put a lily on his chest but Braden's grown, Kieran. A dumbass, but a grown one and he showed up to get it and you gave it to him."

Shaking his head with a deep scowl, Kieran replied, "That's 'cause he didn't know."

"I think he did, deep down. For whatever reason, no matter what she did to him, he held onto it. I mean, he'd carried it around in his wallet for years."

With a serious expression, Kieran questioned, "You ever do something you think isn't that big of a deal and then find out later it could be the worst mistake you've ever made?"

Shrugging at him, Penny shook her head.

"Never mind... Start getting ready, I'm booked for the rest of the day."

Penny gave him a sweet smile before heading over set up his table.

Five

After looking out of his peephole, Seth cautiously opened his apartment door. Apparently it had been muffin week next door. Starting with cherry pecan Monday, the rest of the week had consisted of blueberry, chocolate chip, cranberry almond and mixed berry. His stomach growled as he thought about his hand delivered breakfast over the past week. It hadn't mattered how determined he was not to eat them, half way to work Monday he'd caved in. After taking a bite of the first one, he couldn't stop himself. He'd finished all four before he pulled into the JPT Financial parking lot.

By the time Wednesday rolled around, Penny got the hint and was standing there with the muffins already in a to-go bag. He wasn't sure exactly why she kept giving him muffins but by Friday, he'd smiled back at her and said 'Thanks'. Which was kinda nice, he guessed, but today was Saturday and although he was going for a run, he had nowhere to quickly run off to. If she was there, waiting for him to come out of his apartment, he'd have to talk to her. Just the thought gave him chest pains.

⌘

Penny sat at her kitchen table trying to figure out what to bake for Seth next. The muffins were a hit. Okay well, maybe not. The whole point of giving them to him on a plate was so he would return the plate and she could spark up a conversation with him. After the first two days, it was pretty clear he wasn't going to get chatty. The most he'd said to her was 'Thanks' but he'd sort of smiled when he said it. Maybe he was more of a cinnamon roll type of guy.

Charlotte walked into the kitchen as Penny looked in her book of family recipes.

"Thinking up new ways to stalk the neighbor?"

Laughing Penny replied, "I'm thinking cinnamon rolls..."

"Sounds delicious."

Flipping the recipe book upside down on the table, to hold her spot, she sighed, "I just don't understand it."

"What?" Charlotte asked as she sat down at the table across from Penny.

"I would be excited if someone were baking for me every morning."

"Look, I'm loving the benefits of your stalkery but tasty treats aside, how would you feel if some weird guy was waiting outside your door every morning?"

"But I'm not some weird guy, I'm freakin' awesome and I want us to be friends!" Penny replied getting overly excited out of frustration.

Charlotte stood up with a laugh before saying, "You are awesome. Maybe he's not into baked goods. If the cinnamon rolls don't work, try lingerie."

"Oh ha-ha."

"I bet if he walked out and saw you in your underwear, y'all would be best friends in no time."

"You're not helping," Penny griped.

"Sorry, I forgot you're on the no sex wagon."

Penny giggled at Charlotte's term 'no sex wagon' as she stood up and walked to the living room.

Charlotte followed behind Penny before heading towards the door as she sat down on the couch.

"I'm going to Auggie's I'll see you tomorrow."

Nodding, Penny said, "Okay, see you tomorrow.

As Charlotte left the apartment, Penny looked around. She was happy for her brother and friend but it was a little loncly at the apartment all by herself and in just a few months, she would be living there all alone.

Reaching over to the coffee table, Penny picked up her cell phone and scrolled through her playlist. She needed something to lift her spirits. Swiping past love songs and her 80's rap albums she found just the song. 'Shake it off' by Taylor Swift. Hopping up off of the couch, Penny opened the curtains and front window, allowing fresh air and sunshine to fill the room. She slid her cell phone into the speaker dock against the wall and turned the volume up. Setting the song on loop, that's what she was going to do. She was going to shake it off.

⌘

Swiping his entry card as he jogged back through the security gate that surrounded the apartment complex, Seth admitted the walking path that surrounded the complex was definitely a bonus to living there. It was much better than going to the gym. The humidity was low and the fresh air and sunshine made for a great run. Dashing up the steps to his apartment, he felt relaxed and refreshed.

When Seth reached the balcony, he stopped. His neighbor's window was open wide giving him a direct view of Penny in her living room. Dancing? She was bouncing around, swinging her arms and her long auburn hair was everywhere. He moved to the side a little just in case she turned around. At first he found it hard not to laugh then as he watched her he found himself simply smiling.

He wasn't thinking about how wrong spying on her through the window was until he felt a tap on his shoulder. Pulling his earbuds out of his ears, he quickly turned around.

"Happy Saturday, Lurker!" Liv greeted.

Stumbling back, he couldn't reply. At that moment, Seth wanted to die. Even when Liv winked at him before letting herself into Penny's apartment.

Fumbling for his keys felt like an eternity. When he finally made it in, Seth locked the door and leaned against it. Liv had caught him peeping on Penny. Seth's stomach churned as his head throbbed. He really was a lurker... And he was going to be sick.

⌘

Skipping over to the speaker dock, Penny paused the music on her cell phone. Happy to have the company, Liv was better than any song. Penny had lots of friends, some close and some she just kind of knew but Liv was right there at the top in being one of her favorite people.

Although Liv had married in, Penny always felt like they were closer than any of her cousins. They were sort of in the same boat when it came to the family. Except for the fact that while most of Penny's family disapproved of her life choices, they just plain disapproved of Liv. As far as the older members of her family were concerned, especially Penny's mom Sarah, the men in the family could pretty much do whatever they wanted. They were boys. But God forbid if one of the girls step out of line.

Liv was laughing as she made her way to the couch.

"Don't let me stop you from shakin' that big ol' Irish bootie."

Penny laughed back before correcting, "My bootie's not big but it is very Irish."

"Neighbor boy Lurker seemed to enjoy it," she shared. Practically jumping on top of Liv, Penny hopped onto the couch.

"He was watching me? How? Was he smiling? Did it look like he was going to knock on the door and say hi? Or did he seem..."

"Whoa there! Somethin' going on with you and Lurker?"

Penny slid back and leaned her head against the back couch cushions, saying, "I'm trying to make friends with him."

Slapping her hands together, Liv blurted, "Ha!" before saying, "You are something else, Penny."

"I baked him muffins all last week and the most I got was a 'Thanks' but..."

Liv's eyes grew wide at Penny as she interrupted her questioning, "You did what now?"

With an eye roll as she sighed, Penny explained, "I was trying to be friendly so we could be friends. I baked muffins every morning last week and when he came out to go to work I gave them to him."

"A...."

"Stop looking at me like that!"

Taking a deep breath, Liv shared, "I'm sorry but no one does that. Unless, they're trying to poison someone."

Sitting up straight, Penny gasped, "Oh my gosh!" before asking, "Do you think I should go tell him they're not poisoned?"

Laughing Liv said, "No!"

"Why are you laughing? I don't want him to start thinking I'm crazy! I was going to do cinnamon rolls this week."

Shaking her head at Penny, Liv replied, "You are so sweet and silly. Everyone should get to have you in their life, but he may not want to be friends."

"He wants to be friends, I know it. It's just he doesn't know it yet."

"Just promise you'll stop before you start baking cookies with his face on them."

Penny nodded with a smile. Maybe wooing someone into friendship with baked goods wasn't a common thing but maybe if people did things like that more often, everyone would be happier.

Six

Thankfully Seth had the good sense to stop by the grocery store on his way home from work Friday. He couldn't bring himself to step foot out of his apartment after his run Saturday afternoon. He'd laid in bed all day Sunday with a bag of chips and a jug of water thinking of reasons to move. Then he started making a mental list as to why he should have never moved there in the first place. That led to Seth questioning why the universe hated him enough to place him right next door to the only person, other than his father, that could bring an anxiety attack on just by thinking about her.

Reaching out, for the third time, to open his door, Seth drew in a deep breath and then exhaled leaning his forehead against the door instead of opening it. Surely Penny wouldn't be out there today. There was no doubt in his mind that Liv went straight inside and told her he was watching her through the window.

He had already embarrassed himself enough with her, in one of the most humiliatingly regretful experiences of his life. Now if he gathered the courage to talk to her what was he supposed to say? 'Hey, you know how I took you out that time, didn't speak to you and wouldn't sit next to you? Then had all my classes switched around so I wouldn't have to be anywhere near you? Well, good news neighbor! Now I just peer at you through open windows like a perv'.

The truth was, it had taken Seth nearly the entire school year to work up the courage to go up to Penny and ask her out. He couldn't believe it when she said yes. The night of their date, she looked so pretty in her little yellow sundress. When she smiled and held his hand, it was like holding fresh air and sunshine.

Then her two older brothers walked in and said they needed a word with him out back. Seth knew when they showed him the makeshift cemetery in their back yard it was for pets, not people. The chances of Penny having dated someone named Senior Jingle Bells were slim but it was the fact that her brothers seemed serious.

In his mind, all it would have taken was one wrong move and there would have been a Seth marker right next to Senior Bells. And that's how it usually started. One thought that grew in his mind until it took over the rest of his body, leading to an anxiety attack.

Convincing himself Penny would be too offended by his lurking to be on the balcony with muffins this morning, Seth finally swung the door open and stepped out.
"Good morning!" Penny's voice cheered at him.
Once again, in disbelief, he stared at her.
Titling a large plate towards him, she offered, "Cinnamon roll?"

⌘

Penny's eyebrows raised as she smiled wide in anticipation. Hoping to at least get another thank you out of him, she wasn't prepared for what happened next.

He had a look of sheer panic as he reached back for his doorknob. When he missed, he fell against the wall.
"Are you okay?" Penny asked as he slumped down to the balcony floor.
Unsure of what to do, she stepped closer trying to get a better look at his face and make sure he was still breathing.

With her hands full, Penny nudged his side with her foot, "Umm...Seth?"

Breathing a sigh of relief when he squeezed his eyes shut and groaned, at least he wasn't dead.

"Can I get you something?"

Seth frantically shook his head back and forth as he reached his arm back trying to grab the doorknob.

Doing her best to remain upbeat when it was pretty clear he was trying to get away, Penny asked, "So to go then?"

Continuing to shake his head, Seth choked out a, "No," before finding the doorknob and making his escape.

Penny watched as he flung himself back into his apartment and closed the door.

Standing on the balcony by herself, holding a tray of cinnamon rolls, Penny was about ready to give up. It was one thing for him to be shy, but it was a whole other thing for him freak out and then ninja roll back into his apartment like she was carrying a severed head. It wasn't like she didn't have better things to do then bake goodies for him every morning. She just wanted to be friends. It was getting hard for her not to take his actions personal.

Deciding to give it one final effort, Penny sat down, leaning against the wall between their apartment doors, she placed the tray of cinnamon rolls on her lap. He had to come out sometime and when he did she would just ask him to be her friend. If he said no then, that would be that.

⌘

Lying on the floor by his door, Seth couldn't believe how he had just acted. He thought she would be upset, outraged even but no, she was standing there smiling telling him good morning with freshly baked cinnamon rolls. And he just made a huge ass out of himself.

Picking himself up off of the floor, he knew one of two things was going to happen. One, Penny would not greet him good morning with anything ever again or two, she would still be out there, and he would have to face her. Pulling his cell phone out of the inside pocket of his suit jacket, Seth called his boss.

It only took two rings for Jackson to pick up.
"Hey Seth."
"Jackson, I had something come up this morning. Is it alright if I come in after lunch?"
"I already told you to take a day or two off. Moving is a pain."
"Thank you. I'll be in after lunch."
With a laugh Jackson replied, "Alright then, see you this afternoon," before he hung up.
After taking a moment to appreciate having a man like Jackson as his boss, Seth stepped out of his apartment.

Glancing around, he saw Penny sitting against the wall with the tray of cinnamon rolls on her lap. When she didn't automatically look up at him, he took a few steps closer.
Looking down at his feet, she said, "Oh, you scuffed your shoe."
Before he knew it she had taken a napkin from out of her pocket, put it to her mouth and then started rubbing his shoe with it.
He took a few deep breaths, finding it hard to believe how her touching his shoe was making him feel before saying, "Your cinnamon rolls smell good. May I have one?"
Penny looked up at him and smiled, lifting the tray off of her lap and holding it up towards him.
He started to reach for one, then asked, "Can I sit with you?"
With a little laugh, Penny replied, "It's your balcony too."
Nodding, Seth removed his suit jacket, laid it over the balcony rail and sat down next to Penny.

He sat still next to her for a few minutes without saying a word. After a few controlled breaths, he started to feel more at ease next to her.

Picking up a cinnamon roll off of the tray, he said, "Thank you."

"You're welcome and by the way, they aren't poisoned or anything like that."

Caught off guard, he paused before taking a bite.

Without skipping a beat, she asked, "What do you like to do for fun?"

"Run."

"Really? I don't run unless someone's chasing me," she laughed before asking, "You really like to run? I mean it's fun for you?"

Finishing his bite of cinnamon roll he answered, "Yes I do."

There was an awkward pause before she started talking again.

"I like to hang out with Charlotte and Liv, of course but I like to go out too. Mostly to The Dog House, to watch my brother Braden play and give Auggie a hard time. My brother Ailin used to be in the band. He and Sophia had a baby a few months ago. Then he was offered a promotion at work, they live in Chicago now."

Seth sat there trying to absorb everything she was saying while eating his cinnamon roll.

"You remember Sophia, don't you?"

As he nodded he recalled wondering how someone as nice as Penny could be friends with snotty stuck up Sophia.

"Well anyways, I'm really excited about the fair coming up. Are you?"

Shrugging, he replied, "I guess...No, not really."

Penny appeared disappointed for a moment before asking, "Got any tattoos?"

Seth smiled slightly as he replied, "No."

"Well, if you ever decide to get one, I work at Legacy Ink."

Picking up another cinnamon roll Seth nodded at her before taking a bite.

He remembered that from Charlotte's conversation with his parents. At the time, there seemed to be too much going on for him to dwell on the information but now, he was curious.

"You don't look like you would work there," he shared.

With a little laugh, Penny questioned, "Why? Because I don't look like Liv?"

Feeling a tiny bit embarrassed about his stereotypical judgment, he replied, "Sorry."

Pursing her lips up into a smile, she said, "For all you know, I'm covered with tattoos under my clothes."

Out of reaction, he immediately asked, "Are you?"

Her smile faded as she answered, "No, not even one."

"Why not?" he asked wondering why she seemed sad about it.

"Because it looks like it hurts and they are permanent you know," she replied almost fussing at him like she was defending herself.

"I don't understand why that's a problem..."

With a little sigh, she explained, "I really want to tattoo but my cousin Kieran says he won't teach me until I get one myself."

For reason's unknown to Seth, the idea of Penny as a tattoo artist was the sexiest thing, ever.

⌘

Unsure of why Seth was suddenly staring at her the way that he was, she looked down at the, now empty, tray on her lap.

"Well, speaking of... I better get inside and get ready for work," Penny shared.

Quickly hopping up, Seth held his hand out for hers.

Penny took his hand saying, "Wow, you're strong," as he pulled her to her feet.

He smiled and looked down at the ground before replying, "Thank you for the cinnamon rolls."

Watching him closely, she complimented, "You have a nice smile."

"You have a nice everything," he shared before seemingly realizing what he had just said.
Swiftly grabbing his suit jacket off of the railing, he turned and was back in his apartment with the door closed before she could respond.

Regardless of his speedy exit, Penny considered the morning a great success on her path to making friends with Seth. Sure they seemed to have absolutely nothing in common but she just needed to get to know him better. All in all, it was definitely a step in the friendship direction.

Seven

The rest of the week was a cinnamon roll success as Penny noticed Seth heading out to work a little earlier each day, giving them a chance to visit each morning. He even agreed to come over for dinner one night, 'sometime' but still he agreed. It was a good thing too because honestly, Penny was getting tired of waking up at five to bake for him.

Sitting in the corner of Bitsie's Bridal, Penny and Liv stayed out of the way while Charlotte's mom Amila helped Charlotte into the gown she picked out.

"I don't know why Amila's getting all teary eyed."

Popping Liv on the arm, Penny scolded, "Liv!"

"What? Charlotte's just getting married. It's not like she's moving off to another country."

In a hushed tone Penny fussed, "What is wrong with you?"

Hopping to her feet, Liv snapped, "Nothin'" and headed toward the exit door.

Penny sat there for a moment before she realized why Liv must be upset.

Getting up to go after her, she heard Charlotte ask, "What's wrong with Liv?"

Shaking her head as she walked past, Penny answered, "I think she's sad about her mom."

With an understanding nod, Charlotte said, "Her mom died when she was five," when Amila looked at her with concern.

Feeling bad for Liv, Penny didn't always agree with her own mom but she couldn't imagine her not being there either.

It took Penny a minute to find Liv once she was outside the boutique. Walking around the corner of the building, she finally spotted her.

"Hey!" she said making her way up beside Liv.

Noticeably upset, Liv replied, "I just need a minute."

"I guess you wish your mom had been there when you got married."

After giving Penny a strange look, Liv laughed, "Why? I didn't know the woman at all."

Confused, she questioned, "Isn't that why you're upset?"

"That'd be easier to deal with," Liv replied before sharing, "He won't talk to me."

"Kieran?"

With a loud exhale, she replied, "I've tried everything I can think of to get him to tell me what the problem is and all he says is that it's nothin'." Then waving her finger around she continued saying, "But I know it's something, he barely looks at me."

Recalling what Kieran had asked her at the shop, Penny speculated, "Maybe he feels bad about marking Braden."

"I thought so at first too cause that's when it started but he just gave me his usual spiel about following the rules."

"He has the right to deny or change them if he sees fit, though. That's why it's such a big responsibility. To keep with tradition but there's always exceptions."

Appearing very interested, Liv questioned, "What do you mean?"

"Well, you know there is a marker and a drawer, right," as Liv nodded, Penny continued, "Both positions are passed down although the drawer isn't usually by blood. When Kieran's mom got really sick and knew she wasn't going to make it much longer she passed the title over to my mom. The drawer doesn't have any real control or say so, and there can actually be more than one or not one. The tattoo rests with the sole discretion of the marker."

Holding her hand up, Liv asked, "Wait, are you telling me anyone can draw out the tattoo?"

"Well, yeah. I drew out Auggie's 'cause mom refused and I'm not a 'drawer'. Kieran approved it and he's the marker so..."

Liv was infuriated as she all but demanded, "What happens to the drawing after the tattoo?"

A tad cautious, Penny replied, "They all go in a big log book."

"Where is it?" she snapped.

"It's kept in the marking room, why?"

Slapping the tops of her thighs, Liv blurted, "Son of a bitch, I better be wrong!"

As Liv headed to her car, Penny shouted after her, "Where are you going?"

Without answering, Liv got in her car and sped away.

Penny stood there confused for a minute before heading back into the boutique. She had an idea of what Liv was hinting at but refused to entertain the thought. Kieran took his position as marker far too seriously to mess with tradition like that.

As she walked back into Bitsie's, she started to choke up at the sight of Charlotte. It was almost unreal for someone to look that beautiful.

"This is the one," Charlotte assured with a smile.

Penny glanced over the strapless white satin gown with a peacock blue sash, saying, "It's perfect."

"I still need to pick out my veil but..." Charlotte shared before pausing to ask, "Oh, where's Liv?"

With a slight shrug, Penny replied, "I think she went home."

"Oh-kay."

"She must really be upset," Amila chimed in, noticing Charlotte's irritated expression.

"Yea..." Charlotte mumbled clearly disappointed at Liv's absence.

Giving an apologetic smile, Penny walked back to the corner to sit down while Amila helped Charlotte out of her wedding dress.

⌘

Seth's heart was pounding in his ears along with the music playing through his earbuds. After starting out with long strides, he had picked up the pace, running the walking path around his apartment complex until his body refused to keep going.

What started out as an enjoyable way to clear his head on Saturday afternoon, had quickly turned into a race to get Penny off of his mind. It wasn't that he minded thinking about Penny, in fact, he enjoyed thinking about her. The more he thought about her though, the harder it was to talk to her when they were face to face. It was clear she wanted to be friends. That worked fine for him. She was sweet, funny and so pretty. Not to mention, being friends was a low-pressure way to spend time with her. A lot less is expected in friendship situations. The only problem was when Seth thought about Penny, friendship was the farthest thing from his mind.

Swiping his gate card before jogging through the gate as he headed back to his apartment, Seth faintly heard a horn honk, through the music still playing in his ears. Moving to the side to let the car through, he saw Charlotte and Penny both wave at him as they pulled into the apartment complex. Seth stopped for a second, wishing his run had done him more good before continuing on his way.

He could see Penny sitting at the top of the stairs on their balcony as he made his was closer. The thought of her waiting there for him and what they might briefly talk about before he headed into his apartment to shower gave him a second wind as he sprinted up to their building.

Taking the stairs two at a time he stopped a step below Penny noticing the way the sunlight highlighted the redder strands of her auburn hair as he looked down at her. Her hazel eyes leaned more toward the green side today as they sparked up at him.

As he pulled his earbuds out of his ears, he heard her ask, "How was your run?"

"It was alright," he replied before asking, "How is your day going?"

Without answering his question, she took a deep breath then exhaled before pursing her lips up into a smile.

"Bad day?" he questioned curious as to why she didn't answer.

Penny continued to ignore his question as she stood up and asked, "I'm going to The Dog House tonight, wanna come?"

"Sure," he replied before realizing he just said yes to going out with her.

"Good," she cheered before turning to walk back into her apartment.

Standing there trying to think of something to say, Seth watched her open her apartment door before turning back to him.

"I was thinking about nine but you can knock whenever you're ready to go."

Smiling at her, he said, "Alright," suddenly feeling good about her asking him out.

With a little laugh Penny shared, "Okay, see you later," as she stepped inside her apartment.

Once her door was closed, Seth started towards his apartment when he felt his phone vibrate from his shirt pocket. He pulled it out to see who was calling and just like that all good feelings were gone.

Eight

Standing in front of Penny's door, Seth stared at it for a good ten minutes before knocking. Having his father call and basically order him to attend Sunday brunch at his parent's house had him on edge. He was sure there was an ulterior motive behind it. It had been years since Seth was invited to anything family related, including Christmas.

Focusing on the moment as he waited for Penny to answer the door, he tried to put everything other than tonight out of his mind. He'd decided in the shower that he could stay calm enough not to embarrass himself on the way to the bar. Then after a beer or two he would be relaxed enough to have a nice time with her.

Thinking maybe she hadn't heard him knock the first time, he decided to knock harder. The door quickly swung open and instead of knocking Seth ended up hitting Penny in the shoulder.

"Ow!"

It was pure logic that kept Seth from retreating back to his apartment. If he ran back to his apartment at this point, he'd be the guy that waits for a girl to open the door, and then frogs her in the shoulder and runs away.

"I am so sorry..."

Rubbing her shoulder Penny laughed, "I guess you're ready then?"

Seth quietly nodded.

Penny closed her apartment door and locked it before looking up at him saying, "You can ride with me."

Still in shock at what happened, Seth placed his hand on her shoulder asking, "Are you sure you're okay?"

With a nod, she replied, "I grew up with four brothers. I'm a lot tougher than I look."

Seth allowed his hand to linger on her bare shoulder for a moment before he felt her shiver slightly.

"Sorry..."

Penny slipped on a sweater she was holding before laughing, "It's okay. Just next time let me know we're gonna play punchies."

Well, this was a great way to start the night.

Once they were in the car and heading to The Dog House, Penny broke the awkward silence that had built between them.

"I'm glad you wanted to go with me. I haven't been in a few weeks."

Trying to get semi-comfortable in the passenger seat of Penny's tiny car, Seth replied, "Sure. Hey, is there any way to move the seat back more?"

Penny glanced over and snickered, saying, "You look uncomfortable."

Seth leaned the seat back a bit further, giving himself some relief as he said, "My knees are practically in my chest."

Laughing at him Penny offered, "Next time we can take your car," before asking, "You don't get out much do you?"

"What do you mean?"

"Well, it seems like all you do is go to work."

Feeling put on the spot, he replied, "It's not like there's a whole lot to do here."

"So, no girlfriend then?"

Seth thought for a minute on how to answer that.

He hadn't had a girlfriend since right after he graduated from high school. He'd gone out with a few girls since then, mostly dates arranged by his mother. At first he was too busy between night classes and work then it was just work.

He volunteered to stay late, come in early and even weekends when needed. When he had free time, he went for a run and that was pretty much the extent of his physical activity and social life.

Since he had already been labeled a lurker then earned it by peeping on her and seeing as fifteen minutes ago he practically punched her, he didn't want to add 'weird celibate guy next door' to his ever growing list of shame.

"No, nothing steady."

Shrugging a shoulder at him, she said, "Yea, me neither."

"That's hard to believe," he swore, truly baffled that she was still single.

"It's not like I don't try... It's just that no one ever seems to stick you know."

Seth nodded at her wondering what kind of people she had been with. Who wouldn't want to be with her?

⌘

Penny couldn't help but laugh at the expression on Seth face when they arrived at The Dog House and he was able to get out of her car. He was still stretching his arms and shaking his legs as if they had gone on a ten-hour road trip as she made her way around the car to his side.

As soon as he noticed her standing there, Seth appeared disappointed saying, "I was going to open the door for you."

"Not necessary," she assured heading towards the doors.

Seth skipped ahead of her and quickly pulled open one of the doors.

"After you."

Shaking her head with a laugh, Penny walked into The Dog House.

The bar wasn't too crowded since it was the first night of the county fair, which meant it was free to get in, and most people were there. That is where her brother Braden was supposed to be too. Frowning the second she saw him on stage, singing in the most agonizingly monotone voice she'd ever heard, she caught sight of Brooks playing drums behind him.

Turning back to Seth, she said, "We can get our drinks at the bar and then find a table."

Nodding at her, he replied, "Okay," as they made their way up to the bar.

Not wanting to leave Seth at the bar by himself, she texted Charlotte to let her know she was there.

As they got closer, she noticed Liv sitting at the bar. Penny's brother Auggie was on the opposite side filling drink orders. When she didn't see any signs of Kieran, Penny figured whatever went down between them when Liv left the bridal shop, didn't end well. Liv rarely went out without her husband and if she did, it was with Penny or Charlotte. Stepping next to Liv, Penny nudged her.

Glancing up at Penny and Seth, she said, "Hey," before looking back down into her drink.

Seth tapped Penny on the shoulder before leaning to her ear asking, "Is she okay?"

Turning to him she whispered back, "You know how sometimes people get loud and obnoxious when they have too much to drink?" Seth nodded as she shared, "Liv's the opposite of that."

Continuing to nod, he said, "Scary."

"Yep," she agreed before leaning forward and shouting, "Can we get some service down here bartender?"

Making his way over, Auggie glanced at Seth before greeting, "Hey, Henny Penny."

"Ugh, I hate when you call me that."

"Who's this guy?"

Before Penny could introduce him, Seth stuck his hand across the bar saying, "Seth."

Auggie glared at him for a second before wiping his hand on the towel over his shoulder, and shaking his hand. Penny smiled, thinking 'wow that's a first'.

"Seth... You look familiar," Auggie swore as he continued to stare at him.

"He works for Jackson at JPT."

She could tell Seth was getting nervous by the tone of his voice as he replied, "Yea, I've a... I've talked to you on the phone before."

Auggie placed his hand over his mouth and scowled before running it down the front of his beard saying, "Nah, that's not it."

"Okay well, in the meantime can we get our drinks?" Penny blurted hoping to get away from the bar before Auggie figured it out.

Unfortunately, when Seth reached in his back pocket to pull out his wallet, Auggie slammed his hands down on the bar and shouted, "I got it!"

"Uh..." was the only sound Seth made as Auggie's voice boomed across the bar.

"I got it! You're Boyfriend Graveyard!"
Penny placed her hand across her forehead and shook her head.

While Auggie appeared proud of himself, Seth looked mortified. Almost everyone in the bar had taken notice of Auggie's outburst and were staring directly at Seth standing there with his wallet in his now shaky hand.

"Ah, hell," Auggie laughed, shaking his head before saying, "Put your money away. It's on the house, man."
About that time, Charlotte walked behind the bar. Penny thought maybe things would get better but no, they only got worse.

Giving Penny an excited smile Charlotte greeted Seth saying, "Hey there neighbor."

Auggie's amusement faded into a confused expression as he glanced at Penny, then Seth, then back to Charlotte.

Pointing his thumb towards Penny and Seth, he questioned, "Boyfriend Graveyard is the guy Penny's been muffin stalkin'?"

Penny's eyes grew wide as she watched Charlotte smack her brother in the shoulder.

Completely embarrassed, Penny fussed, "Oh for the love of God! Can we please just get our drinks."

Shaking his head with a laugh, even though Charlotte was glaring at him like she could kill him, Auggie asked, "What can I get ya?"

Seth gave a nod replying, "Guinness."

Auggie quickly said, "Good man," before handing Seth a pint and asking, "Pen, ginger ale?"

Penny noticed Charlotte mouth 'I am so sorry' at her before she took her ginger ale from her brother and gave him a dirty look.

After finding an empty table to sit at Penny quickly slid into a chair before Seth could pull it out for her. She watched him as he stopped next to her, sighed and then took the seat across from her. It wasn't that she didn't appreciate his politeness, she just didn't want to give him the wrong impression. She wasn't looking for anything other than friendship.

Sipping her ginger ale, she noticed Seth take two large gulps from his beer.

Clearing his throat, Seth offered, "I don't have to finish my beer if you want to drink."

"Oh, I don't drink."

Appearing perplexed Seth started to question, "Then why..." when Books interrupt him as he walked up and said, "Hey Penny."

Glancing at Seth first, she looked up at Brooks and replied, "Hey."

Running his fingers through his shaggy blonde hair, Brooks said, "Haven't seen you," pausing to look at Seth before continuing, "lately."

Ignoring the fact that it seemed like he was trying to bring up the day he broke up with her, Penny asked, "So why aren't y'all playing at the fair?"

Without answering her, he questioned, "You didn't think I'd be here?"

The situation started to grow awkward as Penny answered, "Umm, I wasn't really thinking about you."

Brooks eyed Seth again before asking, "Can we talk for a minute."

Penny hesitated before replying, "This isn't a good time."

Suddenly Seth stood up and shared, "I'm going to go."

"No wait," she urged but he was already heading towards the door.

Sliding into the seat Seth had sat in, Brooks raised an eyebrow at Penny and smiled. Penny shook her head at Brooks before hopping up and heading after Seth.

Right outside the bar doors, Penny looked around and saw Seth walking down the street.

"Wait!" she hollered at him causing him to stop.

Seth turned in her direction but stayed where he was at.

"Why are you leaving?"

He just stood there shaking his head at her.

Frustrated, she said, "Well, come on I'll drive you back."

"No thanks, I'll walk."

"But it's like ten miles..."

Shrugging a shoulder at her Seth turned away walking down the street.

Confused as to what his deal was, Penny started to head in the direction of her car to follow him when a familiar and unwelcome brunette walked past her and into the bar. Penny glanced down the street at Seth then back at The Dog House. With a heavy sigh, Penny headed back into the bar. She'd have to wait until later to see what Seth's problem was because right now, her brother Braden was the priority.

Nine

Continuing to shake his head at himself as he walked down the street, Seth couldn't believe he could be that stupid. She had to have brought him out to The Dog House to make whoever that guy was jealous. Why else ask him to a bar if she didn't drink?

The whole thing had been ridiculous to begin with. That must have been her plan all along. No one's that nice unless they want something from you. He should have trusted his instincts and stayed away from her. Liv was right. Penny was nothing but trouble.

⌘

The second Penny entered the bar, she scanned the main area looking for Braden's ex Lily. When she finally caught sight of her, she was shocked to see her standing in front of Brooks. Marching forward, she wanted her out before her brother even knew she was there.

The closer she got to them the more Penny felt like Lily wasn't there to see her brother. With a once over the bar again, she figured Braden was in the back since Brooks had come off the stage.

"You are not welcome here," Penny assured as she stepped next to them.

Brooks appeared regretful as he started, "Penny, I a..." before Lily spoke up.

"Relax Penny, your brother's moved on."

"That's good because you've been moving on since y'all started dating," Penny snapped at her before saying, "That still doesn't explain why you're here. You know you're not welcome in my family's bar."

Wrapping her arm around Brooks' waist, Lily, shared, "I'm not here to see your family."

"I don't care why you're here. Get out." Penny growled before shaking her head and giving Brooks a disappointed expression.

Pulling away from Lily, Brooks said, "Penny, let me explain."

"How could you do this to Braden?"

Brooks' expression was full of remorse as he replied, "She came over one day looking for Braden. I didn't mean for anything to happen."

Lily had a smug look on her face as she informed, "For the record, I told him he could have kept seeing you."

Penny started to feel nauseous as she questioned, "You were sleeping with her while you were with me?"

"Only a few times, but it felt wrong that's why I ended it with you," he swore.
Overwhelmed Penny felt like she was going to be sick.

As she turned to get away from them, she stopped when she ran into someone. Looking up, Penny saw the hurt and betrayal in Braden's eyes as he stared at his best friend and the former love of his life before he wrapped an arm around her.

Braden quietly asked, "You okay, Pen?"
Nodding, she was furious and disgusted but more concerned about him.

Keeping his arm around Penny as if he was trying to protect her, Braden shouted, "Both of you get out!"

Lily looked like she was going to say something then quickly changed her expression as Liv stepped next to her and the entire bar heard Auggie's voice demand, "Everybody out! Bar's closed!"
Penny watched as Charlotte stood by the entrance waiting as groaning customers trickled out of The Dog House.

When all that was left was Penny, Braden, Auggie, Lily, Brooks and Liv inside, Charlotte closed the doors and locked them.

Auggie stood at Braden's side saying, "You are one sorry ass bitch." Brooks looked over at Lily before Auggie clarified, "Don't look at her. I'm talkin' to you."

Trying to defend himself, Brooks said, "I didn't mean to..." before Auggie got in his face questioning, "Didn't mean to what? Cheat on my sister?"

Brooks backed up until he was all the way against the wall, holding up his hands pleading, "Penny, tell him you're not mad."

Liv spouted, "You gotta be kidding me."

"This doesn't have anything to do with you Liv," Lily snapped at her before Liv assured, "You're wrong about that."

Charlotte chimed in, "If you don't kick his ass, I will."

Auggie grabbed Brooks by the front of his shirt and pushed him up the wall saying, "Your call Pen."

Penny looked around then said, "Just let him go, being with Lily's going to be punishment enough."

Disappointed in Penny's answer, Auggie asked, "Braden?"

"Braden, man, we go way back. We're like family."

Looking at Brooks, Braden replied, "Yea, I thought so too."

Lily stepped closer saying, "It's not his fault. I had to do something drastic. I'm all alone. I just want you."

Penny looked at Lily like she was crazy as she yelled, "What kind of sick thrill do you get from messing with my family?"

Patting Penny on the shoulder, Braden stepped right in front of Lily and said, "Get the hell out."

"You don't mean that," she urged looking up at him with a soft smile.

Braden looked her in the eye and swore, "Lily, I don't love you anymore."

Lily gave him an evil look before making a sound like she was offended as she walked to the doors and let herself out.

All eyes fell on Auggie, who still had Brooks up against the wall.

"I hope you're happy with her," Braden said as he turned and made his way back to the stage area.

Auggie slowly let go of Brooks and followed Braden as Penny said, "Let him go."

Brooks stood there for a moment like he had something to say, but shook his head at himself instead and walked out of the bar.

"You okay beautiful?" Liv asked giving Penny a sympathetic look.

Penny nodded then quickly spun around when she heard a crashing sound. She may have been okay but her brother clearly wasn't.

Rushing over with Charlotte and Liv to the stage all they could do was watch as Braden smashed his guitar into Brooks drum kit over and over until there was nothing left of either except for broken pieces scattered across the stage.

Sitting down on the edge of the stage, Braden looked at everyone before saying, "I'm done."

All of the sudden Liv seemed angry as she snapped, "Because of her?"

"It's just not in me anymore," he replied.

Penny looked at them thinking it was strange how Braden and Liv always seemed to know what the other was thinking, before everyone else caught on.

"Wait? You're not going to play anymore?" Charlotte questioned.

Auggie appeared frustrated as he griped, "This is damn ridiculous."

Her heart went out to her brother seeing the defeat in his eyes. After all the years of being hurt and broken over the girl he loved that never loved him back, Lily had finally taken everything from him. And what was worse was that, his best friend had been a part of it, leaving him with nothing.

As Penny made her way closer wanting to comfort him, she stopped when Liv started shouting.

"How are you going to let her take that away from you?"

Everyone was a bit shocked that Liv was having such an outraged reaction. Plus the amount she had to drink before Lily walked into the bar was starting to really show as she stumbled a little as she spoke.

"Gah, you're such a..."

Hopping down from the stage Braden fussed back at her, "What are you gonna say? That I'm a punk, Liv?"

Liv gave him a sarcastic laugh as she informed, "Nope, but it starts with a p."

Penny had to throw her hand over her mouth to keep from laughing.

Then Kieran's voice came from behind them griping, "That's enough Liv."

Liv almost fell as she spun around and glared at her husband.

"It's time to go home."

"Afraid not," Liv replied.

Penny watched the expression on her cousin's face carefully as he seemed sorry but then realized everyone was watching and stood up tall demanding, "Now."

Liv appeared genuinely hurt as she patted his chest saying, "You don't get to tell me what to do."

"Liv," Kieran blurted in a strong tone, as she shook her head and staggered towards the doors.

Penny scowled at her cousin, disappointed in him as she said, "I'll take her home with me," and followed Liv out of the bar.

Every few minutes Seth would check out his peephole to see if Penny was back. At first he was planning to apologize, his long walk home had given him some perspective and he thought he might have overreacted. Then, the longer time went on, the more he became certain his initial observation of the situation at the bar was the correct one. He intended to confront her and make sure she kept her distance from this point on.

After hours of waiting, he saw Penny making her way up the stairs. Swinging his door open, Seth stepped out onto the balcony just in time to see Penny sliding her key into her apartment door.

"I guess you had a good talk?" he questioned in a sarcastic tone.

Penny unlocked her door and opened it without stepping inside as she replied, "Yea, it was great."

"Ha! You did ask me out to make your boyfriend jealous," he blurted proud he had gotten it right.

Coldly turning back to the stairs she rolled her eyes saying, "He's not my boyfriend."

"Sorry it didn't work out the way you'd hoped," he snarked at her.

Penny started to step down the stairs then swiftly turned to him griping, "What is your problem?"

"I am not the one in the wrong here. I don't have a problem except that you were being dishonest with me."

"How's that?"

Seth glared at her. If she wanted him to spell it out for her, that was just fine by him.

"You were just making nice with me so you could use me to get what you really wanted."

Giving him an angry look, she shared, "Okay, here's the honest truth. I was dating the guy from the bar before you moved in next door. It ended the same as all the others. I'm a lot of fun to be around but they're not looking for anything serious. So, when you moved in I thought I would try something different."

"I was a guinea pig for your experiment then?"

Penny's eyes were wide as she shook her head saying, "Wow, you are really self-centered."

"I am not."

"Yea you are. You know, I made an effort to be friends with you. It wasn't easy."

"Oh like things are really that hard for you little miss always happy sunshine."

Stepping closer to him, Penny took a short breath before informing, "Your right. When my dad died suddenly of a heart attack after I graduated, that was a cake walk. And it isn't hard at all to have to hide where I go every day because my mom will never approve of anything I do. It was easy to watch my brother slowly slip away before I lost him last year. Tonight was especially easy seeing one of my other brothers give up on everything because he's let the same girl manipulate him since he was sixteen. Not to mention right now Liv is passed out drunk in my car and I don't know how I'm going to get her inside, but that should be easy too right? And you know what, although it would have been nice to have a friend at the bar with me tonight, I don't need one. Because everything is so effortless for me." Seth just stared at her feeling like the scum of the earth.

There was nothing he could say to make up for how he had acted. Not just tonight either. It suddenly occurred to him that even he had made her life harder than necessary by being exactly what she said he was. Self-centered.

It wouldn't make up for the all the things he'd done wrong, but Seth decided he could do something right to show her that he could be a good friend to her.

"Wait right there," he said before hurrying down the stairs.

Spotting Penny's car in the parking lot, he walked over and opened the passenger door. Catching Liv before she rolled out onto the pavement, he scooped her up and threw her over his shoulder.

Seth carried Liv over his shoulder through the parking lot, up the stairs and to Penny's apartment door.

"Where do you want her?" he asked, as she gave him a confused yet grateful expression.

Pushing the door open farther for him, she said, "The couch is fine."

Walking into her apartment, he slid Liv off of his shoulder and onto the couch before making his way back onto the balcony where Penny was still standing.

Looking down at her, Seth asked, "Can we start over?"

Penny pursed her lips up into a smile as she nodded at him.

Taking a deep breath, Seth held his hand out to Penny.

"Hi, I'm Seth. I am a self-centered jerk with anxiety issues that make me act like an ass when I get around pretty redheads."

Penny looked off to the side smiling wider before she took his hand saying, "I'm Penny. I have a crazy dysfunctional family filled with an insane amount of relatives. And I've been known to stalk handsome neighbors with baked goods."

As they shook hands, Seth questioned, "Friends?"

Penny gave a little laugh as she confirmed, "Friends."

Letting go of her hand, Seth smiled as Penny stepped into her apartment and closed the door. Sliding his fingers across his palm, he liked the way her hand felt in his. As he stepped into his own apartment, Seth felt good about starting over with her. The only problem now was, he didn't want to be just friends.

Ten

Waking up early to go for a run, before attending brunch at his parent's house took a back seat when Seth was awakened by a loud banging outside his apartment. He pulled on a pair of jogging pants and a t-shirt before stumbling to his front door. Rubbing his eyes, he looked out of his peephole. Without being able to see where the noise was coming from, he heard more banging and a loud male voice shouting, 'Open the door' and realized it was coming from next door.

Seth opened his door and saw a dark haired man covered in tattoos banging on Penny's door.

Stepping out onto the balcony, he asked, "Can I help you?"

The man gave him a stupid look and continued his ridiculous knocking.

"Hey!" Seth said taking a step closer.

The man turned and faced Seth, griping, "You got a problem?"

Without hesitating, he replied, "Yea, quit banging on my neighbors' door."

"As soon as my wife comes out I will," the man assured before he started banging against it with the side of his fist again.

Realizing he must be Kieran, Liv's husband, the situation made a little more sense but didn't change the fact that the guy was acting crazy out on the balcony.

"Maybe she doesn't want to come out."

Kieran looked Seth up and down before stepping towards him questioning, "And who the hell are you?"
Before he could answer, they heard a door slam, and Penny was standing on the balcony.

In pajama bottoms and a matching cupcake t-shirt with her hair a mess, Penny stood there with her hand on her hip.

"Stop banging on my damn door!" she shouted at Kieran.

Turning to Penny, Kieran said, "I wanna talk to Liv."

"Then call her on the phone," she practically growled at him.

"Just let me in so I can talk to her," he demanded.

Standing in front of her door, she crossed her arms narrowing her eyes at him and snapped, "You should have been talking to her all along."

"I don't need a lecture Pen."

"What you need to do is get your head out of your ass."

"Open the damn door."

Feeling the need to step in, Seth warned, "Watch the way you talk to her."

Both Penny and Kieran looked at him like he was crazy.

Looking back at Penny, Kieran asked, "Who is this guy?"

"Oh, this is my friend Seth," she replied with a smile.

Reaching his arm out, he said, "Kieran. Nice to meet ya," waiting for Seth to shake his hand.
Shaking his hand, Seth was completely bewildered.

⌘

It wasn't that Penny wasn't on Liv's side. She did find it a little ridiculous after complaining that Kieran wouldn't talk to her, now that he wanted to, she didn't want to hear what he had to say.

Stepping to the side when the door opened behind her, Penny heard Liv say, "Go home."

"No," Kieran insisted.

Liv poked her head out of opening between the wall and the door saying, "Why not?"

Kieran's eyes were soft as he answered, "Because you're not there."

"So?" Liv spouted at him.

Leaning his head down with his voice low, he said, "I'm sorry. I made a mistake."

"Just one?" she snapped.

Resting his head against the door frame, Kieran admitted, "Anything I did that hurt you was a mistake. No matter what mark I have, you're my heart. You're everything to me Liv."

"Can you give us a minute?" Liv asked as she opened the door to let her husband in.

As Kieran closed the door behind himself, Penny shouted, "Okay, I'll just be out here. On the balcony. In my pajamas."

Standing there, she looked around before settling on Seth who was standing there with a puzzled look on his face.

Penny smiled as she thought to herself, 'Welcome to my world'.

"Good morning," she cheered.

Seth smiled back as he shook his head saying, "Interesting morning."

"You should know, as far as Caffrey situations go, that was like a 2 on a scale of 1 to 10," Penny laughed.

Raising his eyebrows, Seth asked, "Really?"

"I feel since we're friends it's only fair to warn you, it gets worse."

Seth glanced back at his door before asking, "Would you like to come in and maybe have some breakfast?"

Caught off guard by his invitation, she replied, "Umm, okay."

"You know, so you don't have to stand out here in your pajamas."

Penny nodded with a smile before following him into his apartment.

Glancing around Seth's apartment, Penny saw a black leather couch against the wall opposite from a medium size flat screen TV on a stand. There was a small square table in the kitchen that looked like it could have been a butcher block with two chairs next to it. And that was about it.

"Are you hungry?" he asked walking into the kitchen.

Without thinking twice, Penny replied, "Wow, it is really boring in here."

Seth quickly turned around and asked, "What?"

"You spend so much time in here, I thought it would be more interesting. Even doctor's offices have pictures on the walls."

"You think my apartment looks like a doctor's office?"

Shaking her head, Penny replied, "No, it's worse."

Seth scowled at her saying, "Oh," before walking back to the kitchen.

Thinking she may have hurt his feelings, Penny followed him and sat down at his table.

Seth pulled three boxes of cereal out of the cabinet and set them on the table in front of her before grabbing a carton of milk. Placing it on the table too, he walked back grabbed a bowl and spoon then set them in front of her.

Pushing the bowl away, Penny crossed her arms against the table asking, "Did I hurt your feelings?"

Seth sat down in the other chair replying, "No."

"Are you gonna eat?"

Shaking his head he informed, "I only have one bowl."

"You're kidding me right."

"I'm the only one that lives here why would I need more?"

Stopping for a moment to think, Penny hopped up from the chair.

She could feel his eyes on her as she opened his silverware drawer. Inside the drawer there was a butter knife and one with a serrated edge, a salad fork and a dinner fork, and a soup spoon. Grabbing the soup spoon out of the drawer, she closed it and walked back to the table.

Sitting back down, she pushed the bowl between them asking, "Which one is your favorite?"

Seth hesitantly pointed to the coco puffs.

"Ah, good choice," Penny complimented as she poured the cereal into the bowl.

After adding milk, she handed him the soup spoon.

"We're sharing," she insisted, urging him to eat.

It took him a few minutes of her nodding and smiling as she ate before Seth decided to share the cereal with her.

Once the bowl of cereal that they were sharing was empty, Penny started to take it to the kitchen when Seth took it from her. He immediately washed and dried it along with the spoons and put them away.

Smiling at him, Penny couldn't help noticing his messy hair. Trying to run her fingers through her own, she started to laugh.

"What?"

"I just realized my hair's not even brushed."

Seth smiled back at her saying, "You do look like you just rolled out of bed."

Nodding at him she shared, "That's because I did."

As Seth continued to smile at her, Penny couldn't help the warm and fuzzy feeling it created inside of her.

Realizing it wasn't a friendly feeling, she said, "I better get back next door."

"Okay," he replied appearing slightly disappointed.

"Thanks for breakfast," she said turning to leave.

When she reached the door and started to open it, Seth asked, "Do you really think it's boring in here."

Giving him a sympathetic expression, she said, "Yea," then smiling she offered, "On the plus side though, if you have a girl over you're definitely the main attraction."

Seth bit his bottom lip as he smiled and looked off to the side as Penny gave him a little wave and walked out.

Taking a deep breath when she stepped out onto the balcony, Penny headed to her apartment thinking, it may not have been the best idea to befriend someone as cute as Seth.

Eleven

Rigid in his chair, Seth waited for his father to speak. When Leonard demanded he come for lunch, Seth had no idea it would be just the two of them. With no buffer or anyone else to concentrate on, he started to feel his chest constricting.

Leonard leaned forward slightly in his chair before questioning, "How much longer do you plan on causing your mother and I this embarrassment?"

"Pardon?"

Appearing put out, his father replied, "I have always tolerated your inadequacies."

Staring at his father, Seth tried to focus on the fact that he did not live there anymore as he felt bile rising in his throat.

"What was it called? Stress induced anxiety?"

"Yes sir," he forced out thinking, 'is' not 'was'.

Leonard stood up and walked to a large china cabinet against the wall.

Looking into the cabinet instead of at his son, he stated, "Your mother is organizing a hospital fundraiser in honor of my father. For some reason, unknown to me, your grandmother feels you should attend."

"Would you prefer that I not?"

Turning away from the china cabinet, his father turned his back on him assuring, "I would have preferred that you had not turned out to be the disappointment that you are."

As Seth's breathing picked up speed he stood, sharing, "I need to go."

When there was no response from his father, Seth walked past him on his way out.

No matter how many times Seth had heard the things his father said to him, nothing dulled the sting of knowing his father didn't care for him.

⌘

There was just enough time for Penny to change out of her pajamas after Liv and Kieran left before Charlotte stormed into the apartment with Auggie right behind her. Wondering if there was something in the air lately, now, they were at it.

"Stop following me," Charlotte griped at Auggie who appeared equally furious.

Without closing the door behind himself, Auggie fussed, "Quit tryin' to run things."

Charlotte appeared offended as she snapped, "It was just a suggestion."

Scowling back at her he swore, "It was a stupid ass one."

Penny rolled her eyes at them and walked towards the door.

Peeking outside, to make sure none of her neighbors were interested in what was going on, this was the second disturbance at her apartment today and the last thing she wanted was for anyone to file a complaint. Just as she was about to close the door, she saw her favorite neighbor making his way up the stairs. Stepping out onto the balcony, Penny pulled her door closed. Not that it helped in any way. Neither Charlotte nor Auggie were quiet or subtle people and when they argued, they always tried to outdo each other.

Wondering if Seth would invite her over again, Penny gave him a sweet smile when he reached the top of the stairs. She noticed him stop and stare at her for a moment before appearing to relax and then smiling back. Just as she was about to ask him how his day was going, the obviousness of how hers was, echoed from inside the apartment.

Penny sighed and shook her head as Seth asked, "I thought they made up."

"Apparently, it's Charlotte and Auggie's turn to argue."

Nodding, Seth asked, "What level are we at?"

"Everything with Auggie is a 5 or higher," Penny laughed just before the door flew open.
Auggie stepped out onto the balcony instantly glaring at Seth.

"You," he growled before questioning, "Should the woman get to make all the decisions."

Penny chanted in her head, 'Don't answer. Please, don't answer' as Seth replied, "No. I thi..."

Turning back to the apartment Auggie shouted, "Ha!" at Charlotte.

Charlotte gave him a sarcastic smile saying, "Alright, forget about what I suggested." Auggie's expression started to soften until she narrowed her eyes saying, "It starts now," and slammed the door in his face.

With a loud frustrated exhale, Auggie glanced at Seth saying, "Let's go," as he headed down the stairs.
In shock, Penny stared at Seth while he looked back at her like he had no idea what to do.

"You comin' or what?" Auggie shouted from the bottom of the stairs.
To her surprise, Seth turned and followed her brother down the stairs, through the parking lot and into his truck.

With a heavy sigh of her own, Penny walked into her apartment to see what was going on.

The second Penny stepped in Charlotte griped, "That man is insane."

She couldn't help but laugh as she questioned, "This something you just figured out?"

Leaning her head back against the couch, Charlotte replied, "I wasn't even being serious."

Penny sat down next to Charlotte asking, "So what happened?"

"Okay, in one of the bridal magazines it said to build anticipation for the 'big night', couples should abstain from sex at least two weeks before the wedding."

Instantly wishing she hadn't asked, Penny stated, "I'm uncomfortable with this conversation," as she started to get up.

Catching her arm and pulling her back down, Charlotte stressed, "Too bad, you're my maid of honor and you have to talk me through things like this."

Penny held up her hand saying, "I swear Charlotte..."

"Anyways, I jokingly suggested we do that and he acted like I was asking to chop his hands off."

Penny was well aware of the fact that her brother and roommate enjoyed each other. She'd even walked in on them once and what she witnessed was incredibly psychologically scarring. The fact of the matter was, friend or not, the subject of her brother and sex was never to be discussed.

Frowning, Penny replied, "Please stop talking now."

Charlotte gave a slight huff saying, "Fine, I'm going to call Liv."

"Thank you!"

As Charlotte stood up and walked to her room, Penny was relieved the conversation was over.

⌘

Twenty minutes into their drive, Auggie pulled down a gravel road that led to an old country house with a wraparound porch. Wondering where they were, Seth hadn't had the nerve to interrupt Auggie's shouting to ask where they were headed. Unsure if Auggie was talking to him or to himself when he banged his palm against the steering wheel saying things like 'That woman is gonna kill me' and 'She is outta her damn mind'.

When they pulled up to the house, Seth saw Liv and Kieran sitting on a porch swing. As they got out of Auggie's truck and headed toward the house, Seth was almost certain Liv was on the phone with Charlotte. She took one look at Auggie, cursed at him and walked inside with her phone to her ear.

Without getting up, Kieran laughed, "What'd ya do?"

Auggie reached down and shook Kieran's hand griping, "Stood my ground," before sitting down on a chair next to the swing.

With a wide smile, Kieran shook his head at Auggie before giving Seth a nod saying, "Pull up a chair, man." Glancing around the porch, Seth found a chair and pulled it closer but not too close to them.

While Auggie and Kieran seemed to discuss what happened earlier that day without giving any details, Seth felt a little out of place. He was dressed to have lunch at his parents' house. Not that it was a whole lot different from what he normally wore, but between his crisp button down tucked into his khaki's with a perfect crease down the center of each leg and dress shoes, he stuck out like a sore thumb. Although Auggie wore a button down also, his sleeves were rolled halfway up his forearm and it looked like it had never seen an iron. And Kieran wasn't even wearing a shirt, making an awkward situation more uncomfortable than it already was.

It wasn't long before Liv came back outside carrying a bottle of whiskey and four glasses. The three of them watched as she walked to the round wooden table next to them.

As she set them in the center of the table, Auggie teased, "Comin' around to our side?"

"Your dumbass brother's on his way," she shared before laughing, "You boys can't hang with me."

"Is that a challenge?" Auggie questioned.

Liv blurted, "Ha!" before saying, "Not with you." Auggie shot her the finger as she winked at him and headed back inside.

Kieran was the first to stand and pull up a chair up to the table before sitting down. After Auggie did the same, Seth followed suit. They sat there silent for a moment. After wondering why they were just sitting there, he assumed they were waiting for Braden when a brown El Camino pulled up next to Auggie's truck. Shuffling up to the house Braden made his way onto the porch. Before he reached the table, Kieran held his hand up.

"Go apologize to Liv."

"For what?"

Kieran shrugged, saying, "Doesn't matter. You pissed her off. Now go apologize."

With a loud sigh, Braden turned and headed into the house as Seth noticed Kieran nudge Auggie and smile.

There was instant shouting and cursing inside the house before Braden ran back out onto the porch. Auggie and Kieran started to laugh.

Seth couldn't help but laugh too as Braden moved his shoulder around complaining, "She hit me with the damn broom."

Their laughter subsided as Braden took notice of Seth and pointed at him with a curious expression on his face.

"Boyfriend Graveyard," Auggie informed before Seth had a chance to introduce himself.

"No way," Braden exclaimed then reached his hand over to shake Seth's assuring, "I'd have been nicer to ya had I known you were gonna outgrow me," with a laugh.

"Seth," he corrected shaking Braden's hand.

Nodding Braden asked, "What brings you here?"

It was a good thing Auggie answered, "He's Penny's neighbor," because Seth wasn't entirely sure.

"Wait. Are you the Seth that works for Jacks?"

"Yes."

"Ah, you're practically family then," Braden announced before asking, "Arc we drinking or what?"

Kieran gave a nod and reached for his glass.

Much like with the chairs, Seth noticed Auggie and Braden waited for Kieran to go first. After he filled the bottom of his glass they picking up their own and passed the bottle around. When Braden set the bottle in front of Seth, he did the same thinking he had never drunk on a Sunday let alone before seven o'clock any day of the week before in his life.

Twelve

At two thirty in the morning, Penny pulled up to her cousin's house. When Liv called and said she was bringing Seth back because everyone else had passed out, Penny offer to come get him. In a way, she was irritated with her brother for stealing away her new friend but on the other hand, it made her happy that Seth had survived a night of drinking with them.

The second she got out of the car, Seth was there to greet her.

Noticeably having had too much to drink, he leaned against the hood of her car announcing, "You're here," then looked back at the house shouting, "Penny's here!"

Liv hollered back from the porch, "'Night Seth," before asking, "You sure you got it, Penny?"

"Yea, need me to take anyone else?"

"Nah, Braden and Auggs passed out on the porch, they'll be fine until morning."

"Thanks Liv. 'Night," Penny said before Liv shared, "Call me when you make it home."
Holding her hand high in the air, she waved before Liv stepped inside her house.

Focusing on Seth, Penny tried to be direct with him but found it hard to be serious while he kept smiling at her.

"You're pretty drunk."

Nodding at her, he stumbled closer saying, "You're pretty...Pretty."

Clearing her throat as she smiled at him, Penny replied, "I need you to get in the car so I can take you home okay."

"I can't."

With a little laugh Penny questioned, "You can't?"

Holding out his hands, he answered, "I lost my keys."

"How did you do that?"

With a deep inhale, Seth stood up replying, "Playing freeze tag."

"I don't even want to know how that got started... Can you make it to the passenger side?"

Turning quickly, Seth had to brace himself against the car for a moment before he was steady enough to make it to the other side of the car.

On the way to their apartment complex, Penny noticed Seth starting to drift off.

"Hey, you need to talk to me, so you don't pass out."

Leaning his head toward her, Seth smiled saying, "Anything you want."

A little surprised at how articulate Seth was while drunk. He was over annunciating practically every word but to her, it made the fact that she couldn't look at him while driving a non-issue because she could understand every word. Pausing for a moment to consider it was sort of wrong to take advantage of his intoxicated state, her curiosity made it impossible for her to resist.

"What did you think of my family?"

Suddenly very alert, Seth grabbed her shoulder blurting, "Did you know Kieran has a legacy?"

"Um... yea," she replied.

"That goes back generations?"

Laughing, she asked, "How'd you get along with Auggie?"

Giving her a strange look he replied, "He called me...Cara"

"A chara?"

"That's it."

That made Penny happier than it should have as she explained, "He was just saying you're a friend."

Seth laughed as he shared, "Much better."

"And Braden?"

"He thinks Charlotte's hot."

Shaking her head Penny laughed saying, "I'm sure he does," knowing Braden said it to aggravate Auggie.

"I don't."

"No?"

Seth lowered his voice, almost whispering, "Kieran said it's because I have a thing for Penny."

Penny was speechless.

On the one hand, how could she not ask and find out for sure. On the other hand, Penny wasn't entirely sure she wanted to know the answer. Her idea of making friends with him wasn't to end up with him. Honestly, she was leaning towards the smitten side herself but that didn't change the fact that they were neighbors. If she did let it go farther, when the inevitable happened, she would still have to face him every day. No, friend's was what they were and that was all they were going to be.

Parked in the apartment complex parking lot, Penny got out of the car and walked around to the passenger side.

Opening the passenger door, Seth swung his legs out saying, "I need to lay down."

"Okay just a minute. You're doing good. All you have to do is make it up the stairs," she said watching as he placed his head in his hands and rested his elbows on his knees.

He started to shake his head as he leaned forward.

Moving directly in front of him, she placed her hands on his shoulders to brace him saying, "No, no. You can't pass out in the parking lot."

Penny had to take a deep breath when he wrapped his arms around her waist and leaned into her.

Seth sat halfway out of the car holding onto her without moving or making a sound. She started to wonder if he had passed out.

"Seth?"

Without answering, his hands gripped the back of her shirt as he tugged her closer.

"Seth."

All thoughts of friendship were drifting away. As much as she would have liked to relax and move even closer, Penny reminded herself he was drunk.

His voice was smooth and low as he lifted his head and looked up at her saying, "Anything you want."

"Please don't do this to me," she whispered.

Seth stared at her for a long moment before letting go.

The second she stepped away, he held onto the car door and stood up. When she reached for his arm, to help him, Seth took off towards the stairs. Penny stood at her car watching him walk the short distance to the bottom of the stairs. In the moment she didn't want to turn him down but what choice did she have. He probably wouldn't remember anything tomorrow anyway. Still the look on his face, like he had been lost and finally found what he was looking for, was something she would never forget, no matter what.

Thirteen

Pulling a blanket over his head as he rolled over, Seth couldn't recall his couch being this comfortable or having a blanket. Pressing his head against the couch cushion, he didn't have to open his eyes and look around to realize he wasn't in his apartment.

Events from the previous day and night rolled through his mind. That was the most fun he'd had in his entire life. It wasn't like he'd never been drunk before but it was more than drinking. It was being laughed at and laughing back. Playing elementary school playground games, which is harder than you would think after several glasses of whiskey. Then as he heard a familiar laugh come from another room, Seth recalled his ride home with Penny.

Why in the world would he tell her what Kieran said? Now understanding what Auggie meant when he said 'whiskey'll make a honest man of ya', he wondered if it made him an idiot too. Mentally scolding himself he thought, 'Anything you want'. Who says stuff like that? Not to mention the fact that it made no sense. Sure the first time he said it, he was answering her. But when she was looking down at him like he was he only man in the world, that was his response. All the things he could have said and 'anything you want' was what came out of his mouth.

In the back of his mind, he was hoping Penny would tap him on the shoulder and say she was leaving and he could let himself out. He was off because of the holiday but he doubted a tattoo shop would be closed for it. If she needed to go to work and he appeared to still be sleeping, that would have been ideal. It would have been so much better than Liv pouncing on top of him.

"Rise and shine, Lurker!" she announced, patting him on top of his blanket covered head.

Feeling her push away from him, Seth peeked out from under the blanket at her.

"I found your keys in the yard, they're on the table."

Grateful for that, at least he wouldn't have to deal with Marty to get his apartment unlocked. He watched Liv turn and walk to the front door where Charlotte was standing.

"Thank you," he appreciated.

Liv and Charlotte looked at each other before teasing in unison, "Anything you want."

As they left, Seth pulled the blanket back over his head and groaned.

⌘

Feeling a bit nervous Penny sat at her kitchen table waiting for Seth to come in and get his keys. She knew he was up, she had heard his voice. Since Charlotte and Liv ruined her plan of pretending what was said last night never happened, she wondered if he remembered too and that was what was taking him so long.

Growing impatient, she felt the need to get all awkwardness resolved so they could go back to normal. Well, normal for Seth. Just as she was about to get up, he stepped into the kitchen.

"Morning," she cheered at him glancing over his 'just rolled out of bed' appearance, even though he'd been on her couch.

Taking a step closer, Seth gave a shy smile. There were what appeared to be grass stains on his otherwise white undershirt, his hair was messy and his always perfectly creased slacks were full of wrinkles.

"Thank you for the ride home."

Pursing her lips up into a smile, she asked, "How ya feeling this morning?"

He paused for a moment before replying, "Not too bad."

Hopping up, she said, "Have a seat," before asking, "Coffee?"

"Yes please."

With a sweet smile, Penny was happy he wasn't rushing home as she walked over to pour him a cup of coffee.

⌘

Watching her sweep her hair over her shoulder as she poured his coffee into a cup, Seth thought about her long hair spilling over her shoulders and falling against him as she looked down at him the night before. He wasn't trying to come on to her, but it was hard to resist the feeling of being close and wanting to get closer. He wanted to wrap his fingers in her hair and pull her in. Kiss her. It wasn't having too much to drink last night that caused him to feel that way. Right now, in her kitchen slightly hung over with sunlight pouring through the windows, he wanted her even more.

As Penny returned to the table with his cup of coffee, Seth decided he needed confirmation on her part before moving forward. After all, in his intoxicated state the previous night, he could have completely misjudged her reaction to him.

"Cream and sugar?" she asked, setting the cup down in front of him.

Thinking of her naturally beautiful complexion and the fact that she was sweeter than anyone he'd ever known, Seth replied, "Yes," as he mentally added 'You are'.

Penny reached toward the center of the table to retrieve them for him at the same time he did, giving him the opportunity to touch her hand. Running the pad of his thumb against the top of her hand, he glanced over to see her reaction.

"Hey! Pen-Pen!" startled them both before they heard the front door slam shut.

Penny stood up straight tucking her hair behind both ears as she gave him a soft smile before turning away.

Braden walked into the kitchen looking pretty much the same way he did when he showed up at Kieran's the day before.

Slapping Seth on the back as he pulled out a chair, he greeted, "How's it goin'?"

Before Seth could answer Penny placed her hand on her hip questioning, "What are you doing here?"

Flashing a wide smile, he replied, "What? I need a reason to visit my favorite sister?"

Rolling her eyes at him she said, "Usually, and I'm your only sister."

"That doesn't make it any less meaningful," he assured.

Laughing, Penny asked, "Why are you here?"

Taking a seat, Braden answered, "I'm kinda homeless right now and I was hoping you'd let me crash here for a while."

With a miserable expression, Penny suggested, "Go stay with mom."

"Do you just hate me?"

"You can have my old room," she teased with a smirk.

Giving her a pleading look, Braden begged, "Come on, you know if I stay at Auggie's we'll be fighting the whole time and Liv's crazy mad at me so I can't stay at Kieran's. Please."

"Alight," Penny sighed before informing, "But you have to ask Charlotte too."

Like he was proud of himself, Braden blurted, "Sweet!" before leaning back in the chair asking, "So what's for breakfast."

Leaning her head back, Penny made an irritated noise before walking out of the room.

Sipping his coffee, Seth enjoyed listening to Penny and Braden's exchange. He'd always wondered what it would have been like to have siblings.

As he started to wonder if that would have taken some of the pressure off him growing up as an only child, he heard Braden ask, "You stay here last night?"

Unsure what was going to happen next, he replied, "Yes."

Nodding, Braden questioned, "What's up with you and Penny?"

"I moved in next door and she kind of befriended me," Seth replied feeling like he should smile at the thought.

"Makes sense, she has a thing for losers."

Slightly offended, he said, "Okay."

Laughing Braden slapped Seth's arm, clarifying, "Not you, man," before informing, "That y'all are friends. She's mostly into guys that hang around the shop because they don't work and piece of shit drummer's that'll screw just about anyone."

Nodding, Seth couldn't help being a little disappointed. Clearly he wasn't her type.

⌘

Standing in her room, Penny needed a moment. It was actually a good thing Braden showed up when he did because when Seth touched her hand with that curious look in his eyes, she could feel herself starting to give in. Mentally reminding herself, 'Only friendship feelings' she did her best to put wanting him to look at her the way he did last night out of her mind.

Focused and determined to keep her overly friendly feelings for Seth at bay, Penny left her room and walked into the living room to find her brother stretched out on the couch.

"Where's Seth?"

Without opening his eyes, Braden said, "He went home."

"Oh," Penny sighed, wishing he had hung around a little longer.

Keeping his eyes closed, he shared, "He likes you."

Wishing his eyes were open so he could see the mean look she was shooting him, Penny sneered, "Of course he does, we're friends."

A wide smile spread across his face as he informed, "You like him too."

"No I don't," she insisted.

"Why not? Thought y'all were friends."

Knowing her brother would eventually get the truth out of her if the conversation kept going, Penny snapped, "Shut up, stupid," and walked back to her room.

Fourteen

After having Braden living in the apartment, monopolizing the couch, and Auggie being there every day when Charlotte woke up, until it was time to open the bar, Penny finally had Thursday night all to herself. Liv was still mad at Braden but had calmed down enough to have him over for their weekly pizza and beer night. Her plan for the evening was to make a few more batches of cotton candy lip balm for the last weekend of the fair. Then, she was looking forward to taking a nice hot bath, curl up on the couch and watch a movie.

She had barely seen Seth all week and guessed he was busy. Otherwise, she would have asked him over. Both Auggie and Braden seemed to like him which was nice but she was hoping he would be her friend instead of theirs.

It was probably nice for Seth because she was pretty sure he didn't have any friends but if that was the case she would still be left at square one, after Charlotte and Auggie got married. Not to mention if Braden was still staying with her, she would need a friend.

Although Penny loved her brother, he was not easy to live with. He was messy, never picked up after himself, didn't cook, wouldn't wash a dish or his clothes. Growing up under the same roof with him was enough to have lasted her a lifetime. She swore if he used the term 'woman's work' one more time in her presence, she was going to have to throat punch him.

Waiting for her lip balms to set up on the table, Penny cleaned up after herself before heading out of the kitchen. Ready to lose herself in bubbles and warm water, she stopped in the middle of the living room. As she mentally pleaded, 'Don't be Braden. Don't be Braden' she stepped over to the door.

To Penny's pleasant surprise, Seth was standing on the other side of the door when she looked out of the peephole.

Opening the door, she cheered, "Hi!"

Seth looked down at his feet asking, "Can I come in?" Nodding she let him in, wondering if something was wrong.

"Is everything okay?"

"Would you like to go to the fair?" he questioned, appearing nervous.

Trying her best to think clearly while her insides were doing summersaults, she asked, "When?"

"Now or tonight...Tonight," he replied seemingly unsure of himself.

Penny hesitantly asked, "On a date?"

Seth looked like he was going to say something and then paused before answering, "As friends."

Relieved and disappointed at the same time, she smiled, saying, "Okay, wait here. I'll just go change and then we can go."

⌘

Seth stood in Penny's living room silently admonishing himself for being a complete and total wuss. He could have said 'yes' and she may have said 'okay'. If she hadn't then, he could have offered to go as friends. Now he would never know what she might have said because he took the safe route.

It wasn't long before Penny walked back into the living room. Seth noticed she had a slight bounce to her walk. It was almost like she wanted to skip but was holding herself back. Smiling at Penny and her cheerful nature he envisioned her skipping everywhere she went.

"I guess we're taking your car," she said in teasing tone.

Wanting to reach down and hold her hand, he nodded, replying, "It would be nice for my legs not go numb."

With a little laugh, Penny nodded back.

Seth wanted to stare at her but kept his eyes focused on the road instead. She was unusually quiet. Glancing at her every chance he could, he knew something was different. Maybe she was upset he hadn't really spoken to her since Sunday. He had purposely avoided her but it wasn't because he didn't want to talk to her. The truth was, he was trying to work up the nerve to ask her out.

It had become easier to talk to her as he got to know her better. However, the second he let his mind wonder or dwelled too long on the fact that less than a week ago he had his arms around her, panic would set in.

Knowing the type of guy Penny was accustom to, thanks to Braden, boosted his confidence enough, where she was concerned, to invite her out. Obviously she didn't know what it was like to be with someone who would treat her right. Someone who knew she was unique and one of a kind. Seth wasn't sure if he was that guy either but he wanted her and although a 'friend date' wasn't what was on his mind, it was definitely a step in the right direction, maybe.

Surprised that Penny waited for him to open the passenger door for her when they arrived at the County Fair, he started to feel hopeful about where the night might lead. He resisted the urge to take her hand by reminding himself of the awkward expression she had on her face when she asked if this was a date.

As they headed to the entrance, Penny asked, "What do you wanna ride first?"

"I don't ride rides," he replied in an apologetic tone.

"Oh."

"Do you want to walk through the livestock?"

Scrunching up her face at him, Penny shared, "I don't like farm animals."

Thinking to himself, 'Yea the fair was a great idea' Seth offered, "Would you like to walk around and get a bite to eat?"

Nodding, Penny smiled as she replied, "Sounds good."
Relieved they reached a compromise, he quickly stepped up to the booth and bought both their tickets just in case she planned to argue about it.

Seth held back a smile as Penny noticeably held her breath through the livestock area when they entered the gates.

Once they made it to the concession area, she took a deep breath and hopped in front of him, saying, "Food's on me."

"No, I invited you out. I'm paying," he replied in a serious tone.

Placing her hand on her hip, Penny fussed "When I go out with friends, they don't pay for me."

A bit frustrated with her, he fussed back, "Well, I didn't want to go out as friends," before thinking it through.

Scowling at him she took a step back asking, "Then why did you say you did?"
Taking a look around to see people staring at them as he realized they were arguing in the middle of the concession area, he said, "Let's get something to eat and sit down."

"No," she snapped before assuring, "I'm not doing anything with you until you answer me."

As the embarrassment of everyone staring started to set in, Seth lowered his voice as he informed, "You're making a scene."

"You want me to make a scene?" Penny raised her voice.

"Seriously, Penny," Seth stressed through gritted teeth.

Shaking her head at him, she argued, "No, you lured me out under false pretenses."
Seth couldn't believe she was doing this to him and in public.

The longer he stood there staring at her the madder he became. Who gets upset because someone wants to pay? All of the sudden the crowd around them no longer mattered to him. This was getting settled right here right now.

"If I had said this was a date you would have said no, then?"

Glancing off to the side, Penny replied, "I don't know," before griping at him, "It doesn't matter because you tricked me."

Offended that Penny was now accusing him of ridiculous things, he protested, "You stalked me for an entire week but I'm the one that tricked you."

"To be your friend!"
Her words stung as Seth grasped what was happening and looked at the situation from her point of view.

He couldn't help feeling stupid and a bit like a jerk. Penny wanted to be friends. She had been fairly clear on that matter all along. Friends and that was it.

Softening his expression, he apologized, "I'm sorry you feel like I misled you, I'll take you home."

Frowning at him, Penny shook her head, saying, "I'll find a ride," before she turned and walked away.

⌘

Making her way to one of the concession booths, Penny felt like she could cry. It was too much. He was too much. She didn't want to consider herself responsible for their argument, but it was sure starting to feel that way.

If he had just let her buy their food, she would have felt better about going out with him. It would have put her back on even ground. Already it had felt like a date and that was not what she wanted. Okay, she did want that but she didn't want the end result of dating, which every experience she'd ever had taught her that the only thing dating led to was breaking up.

Stepping to the Smokin' Hot Legs concession stand, Penny smiled at the lady inside the booth.

Laying her money on the counter, she requested, "One turkey leg, please."

"Sure thing darlin'," the woman replied before stepping back, opening a large ice chest and grabbing a large foil wrapped turkey leg out of it.

The smell of smoked turkey was heavenly as the lady handed Penny a stack of napkins and her turkey leg.

Taking her turkey leg and napkins, she cheered, "Thank you!" before turning and walking toward the covered eating area.

After waving hello to a few people she knew, she found an empty picnic style table and sat down.

The delight in eating something that only came around once a year had dwindled into a feeling of 'I might as well eat' as she sat there by herself. 'Stupid Seth', Penny thought as she set her turkey leg down and started to pout.

⌘

Keeping an eye on Penny as she sat at a table by herself, Seth planned on keeping his distance until it appeared she was ready to go. He wasn't about to leave her there to find a ride home.

He watched as she laid napkins out preparing to eat. She started to unwrap her turkey leg, and then stopped. When Penny swept the entire length of her hair over her shoulder in order to hold the bottom in one hand while brushing her finger across the ends with the other, he could no longer keep his distance.

Making his way in her direction, he noticed her lips barely moving as she scowled at the ends of her hair. It looked like she was talking to herself. As he stopped for a moment to gather his thoughts, Seth wondered if she was thinking about him. Of course she was. She was probably thinking about what a jerk he was. He was a jerk. There was something about her that pushed every one of his buttons, good and bad. For a second, he considered marching over and telling her with all her cheerfulness and persistent befriending, she had disrupted his entire life. Thoughts of what his life was like before he moved in next door to her filled his mind as he started towards her again.

In just a few weeks, Penny had disrupted his life but in the best way possible. He didn't want to go back to his boring life. Seth wanted stupid arguments and not knowing what was going to happen when he stepped out of his apartment each morning. He wanted long Saturday afternoon runs with only her on his mind. The way she instantly brightened his day when all he could think about was how his father turned his back on him. Seth craved the anxious feeling of holding back when he thought of where touching her again might lead. And he wasn't willing to let a simple trip to the fair take all of that away.

Penny instantly dropped her hair and stared at him as he sat down across from her at the table.

"I only invited you here because you said you were excited about it. I hate the fair. I like you Penny, and I don't mean to be a jerk. I'm a really nice guy but when I'm nervous my mind gets carried away, and I end up acting like an ass with you."

An apologetic expression coated her face as she replied, "Now I feel bad."

"You shouldn't," he assured, thinking how sweet she is.

Shrugging a shoulder at him, Penny shared, "If you had moved next door seven or eight month ago, we probably would be on a date right now."

He thought for a moment before asking, "Because of the drummer?"

With a heavy sigh, she replied, "And every other guy I've been with."

Seth wanted to be sympathetic but couldn't help feeling that was unfair to him.

"You know, we can be friends if that's all you want. But it is wrong for you to judge me for things other people have done without giving me a chance to show you I'm different."

Appearing as though she wanted to smile, she offered, "Since we're both already here and I did ride with you, we can still walk around if you want."

"I would like that."

Penny smiled at him before grabbing her turkey leg and napkins off of the table as she stood up.

Finding the preparation and overall sanitary quality of fair food questionable, Seth declined when Penny offered him some of her turkey. Picking pieces off as they walked around the fairgrounds, she insisted on offering him each piece before placing it in her mouth and assuring him it was delicious.

Even though the carnival area was crowded, Seth didn't mind. The lights from the rides provided a pleasant glow now that it was dark. It would be the perfect time to reach over and hold her hand, but they were both occupied by the turkey leg. While he waited for her to finish, Seth decided to be proactive and see what he was really up against.

"What type of guy are you interested in?"

Stopping, she looked up at him asking, "What do you mean?"

"Don't most girls have a list or something?"

Appearing confused, Penny replied, "Do they?"

"Or a preference..."

Shrugging she informed, "It's not that complicated for me. If a guy asks me out and he's not creepy I usually say yes."

"So nothing specific just a man with a pulse?"

Giving him an absurd look, she bumped him with her shoulder before walking again.

Guessing no type was good, the fact that she said yes to almost everyone but no to him was disappointing.

As Seth tried to think of questions that would be more helpful to him, Penny asked, "What about you? What's your type?"

"Would it be incredibly lame if I said you?"

With a slight giggle Penny answered, "Yes, very cheesy."

"Well, the first girl I had a crush on looked just like you."

Penny turned her head to the side trying to hide her smile before asking, "Why don't you have a girlfriend?"

Starting to feel uneasy, he replied, "I just don't."

Penny gave him a suspicious expression as she questioned, "You're not a one night stander are you?"

"No."

With a doubtful look in her eyes she said, "Have you ever had a girlfriend?"

"I had one once but it didn't work out."

"How many women have you slept with?"

Hesitating, Seth wondered if he should make up a number or if he should be honest with her.

Honesty overruled the alternative as he replied, "Two."

Relief washed over him when all Penny did was nod in response, instead of asking how long it had been.

"What about you?"

"Nine."

Seth throat constricted as he choked out, "People?"

"It'd be weird if it wasn't..." Penny laughed as if it was not a big deal at all.

He couldn't help verifying, "Nine?"

Rolling her eyes, she replied, "Over a span of ten years. It's not like I did them all in one night."

Thinking of it in terms of one guy a year helped a little as he said, "I didn't mean to..."

"Oh! Technically it's seven because the first two we didn't actually have sex but we..." before he cut her off assuring, "Alright, that's good. I don't need to know anymore."

With a peculiar expression on her face, Penny nodded then looked away.

⌘

Feeling a bit perturbed with him, he wouldn't have liked it if she had made fun of him for having only slept with two people. Granted nine did sound like a lot, but it really wasn't when you put it into the proper context and chances are if she was a guy, he'd probably have high-fived her.

Looking down at her picked clean turkey leg, Penny took the opportunity to toss it in the next trash can they passed.

"So why didn't it work out?"

Clearing his throat, he shared, "I wasn't what she wanted me to be."

Something felt vaguely familiar about only having one girlfriend and not many partners. Penny thought it best to make sure Seth wasn't a pervert.

With a heavy sigh, she questioned, "Ah, you're not into porn are you? Cause I dated this one guy and..." trailing off when she noticed his eyes grow wide.

Shaking his head at her, he swore, "No and I don't need to hear that story."

Now wondering if he leaned more to the prudish side, she asked, "What did she want you to be?"

"A doctor."

"That's kind of a lot to ask of someone you're dating," she shared, thinking that was an odd reason to break up with someone.

With a half-hearted smile, he confessed, "To be fair, all of the men in my family are doctors."

"I see."

Shrugging, he explained, "It isn't that I wanted to disappoint everyone."

Seeing the distress in his expression, Penny slid her hand into his, assuring, "Just because you're not doing what's expected of you doesn't mean you're wrong for choosing your own path in life."

Tightening his hand around hers, Seth replied, "Someone should tell my father that."

"Well after someone talks to him maybe they could sit down and explain it to my mom."

Penny couldn't help but laugh when she realized of all the things they could have had in common disapproving parents was it.

Fifteen

Feeling inspired when she woke up, Penny hopped out of bed. Her night at the fair with Seth had done more than give her full body tingles when she went to bed. It had helped her make a long overdue decision about her life.

On the way to work, Penny couldn't get over how something as simple as holding his hand made her feel. She actually couldn't remember the last time she'd held hands with a guy, most likely high school. When they had said goodnight right outside her door and he didn't even try to kiss her, she felt an innocence inside her that had long since been gone. She still wasn't sure about dating him but since last night was different than any date she'd been on, the possibility that this was something else started to settle in. Besides, as slow as he moved, they would remain friends long before anything really got started.

As Penny skipped through the doors of Legacy Ink, she couldn't help smiling wide when she saw Kieran standing behind the counter with Liv right by his side.

"Somebody's in a good mood," Liv announced as Penny made her way towards them.

When Penny reached the counter, she laid her arm on top of it.

Smiling up at Kieran, she pointed to the inside of her wrist informing, "I want a double heart right here."

Kieran had a serious expression on his face as Liv congratulated, "That's my girl!"

"I'm ready," Penny cheered at Kieran before he questioned, "You sure you don't need a little more time?"

Liv quickly snapped, "You made a deal with her. She's ready. Now get over there and tattoo her."

Kieran stood still for a moment scowling before noticeably swallowing hard as he nodded.

Excited and nervous, Penny skipped over to Kieran's station and seated herself in the chair.

⌘

Sitting in the conference room at JPT Financial, Seth picked at his ham and cheese sandwich. He was having trouble focusing. He'd missed seeing Penny that morning just like he'd missed his opportunity to kiss her last night. There was something between them, he could feel it when she held his hand, but for some reason when he told her goodnight, the timing felt off. Rubbing his fingers against the palm of his hand, he thought about her hand inside his and how comforting it was. It was as if she sensed what he needed.

From out of nowhere he felt someone slap the back of his shoulder. As he quickly turned, he saw Braden hop onto the conference table.

"What's up, man?" Braden greeted, sitting on the table to his left.

"Hey," Seth replied, curious as to what he was doing there.

Nodding and smiling, Braden asked, "Did ya hear?" As Seth shook his head, Braden shared, "Penny got a tattoo." Seth felt his face grow warm, hoping her brother couldn't tell his heart was now thundering in his chest.

"We're goin' out to Kieran's tonight. You in?"

Moving to the edge of his seat, Seth nodded saying, "Sure."

Sliding off of the table, Braden blurted, "Sweet!" before saying, "I gotta go talk to Jacks. Later, man."

As Braden left the conference room, Seth stood up and discarded his uneaten sandwich.

Hoping Penny was part of the 'We' that were going out to Kieran's, Seth was motivated to go back to his desk and get his work day over as quickly as possible.

⌘

Although her wrist was sore, Penny was thrilled with the new addition to her skin. It was simple and beautiful. She couldn't wait to be back in the shop Monday morning learning to beautify others with ink.

Walking into her apartment, she saw Auggie and Braden sitting on the couch. Auggie appeared irritated while Braden looked like he'd been laughing.

"Something going on?" Penny asked.

Before either of them could answer, Charlotte rushed into the room, demanding, "Let me see!"

With a feeling of pride, Penny pulled the bandage that she had been wearing since this morning off of her wrist and held her arm out for Charlotte.

"Aww... It's so pretty," Charlotte complimented before turning to Auggie as she coaxed, "Isn't it."

Penny felt a little nervous as Auggie stood, stepping over to get a good look, Penny asked, "What do you think?"

Giving her an approving smile, he replied, "It looks nice."

Smiling wide at him, her joy was quickly squashed by disappointment as Braden stood saying, "We'll see ya later, Pen."

"Wait, I thought we were all going to Liv's..."

Auggie's agitated expression, quickly returned as he made a growling noise under his breath, turned, walked to the door and out of the apartment.

Huffing at her fiancé's actions, Charlotte made a face at Braden and informed, "Somebody asked Jackson if he

111

could work behind the bar at The Dog House until he finds another job. So Auggie's training him tonight."

Wearing a wide smile, Braden left the apartment.

Shaking her head at the sheer insanity of her brother and Jacks, Auggie and Braden working together was a terrible idea.

"They can't work together."

"I know. I doubt they'll make it through tonight without getting into a fight."

Nodding Penny agreed saying, "You know I'm starting to think Braden likes inviting trouble into his life."

Laughing a little, Charlotte shared, "He needs a girlfriend."

"And his own place."

Nodding, Charlotte replied, "Why did I agree to let him stay here again?"

"Because, he has that goofy smile that no one can say no to."

"Yea, he's a charmer," Charlotte laughed before saying, "I better go before they kill each other before we even get to the bar."

"Alright."

Penny smiled as she gave a little wave before heading to her room.

Sitting on her bed, she stared at her wrist for a while before changing shirts and walking back into the living room.

"Oh! Hey," she blurted, surprised to see Seth standing there.

Pointing to the door, he said, "Charlotte said to just go in and they would meet us out at Kieran's later."

"You're coming with me?" she asked, trying to hold back how excited she was.

Seth's face fell as he replied, "Braden invited me but I don't have..."

"No," she cut him off before assuring, "I want you to."

"Congratulations on your new career, by the way," he said eyeing her wrist.

As Penny watched him slowly smiled at her, she thought 'This has got to be the best day ever'.

⌘

On edge the entire way out to Kieran's, Seth felt welcomed when he came with Auggie but had no idea how he would be perceived when he showed up with just Penny.

When they arrived, Kieran was sitting on the porch.

As Seth and Penny made their way onto the porch, Kieran greeted them saying, "How's about ya Seth? Pull up a chair," and, "Liv's, inside."

Waiting for Penny to go inside before pulling up a chair, he sat down.

"You and Penny, huh?" Kieran questioned with a 'Careful how you answer' expression on his face.

"That's what I'm hoping," Seth replied.

"Want some advice?"

Wondering if 'stay away from her' was going to be the next thing out of his mouth Seth nodded.

"Penny's been with different versions of the same loser type guy since she started dating. Do you know why?"

Seth shook his head.

"Because they come onto her. Penny doesn't understand beating around the bush. Do you see what I'm saying?"

"I'm not sure."

"I'm not tellin' ya to hook up with her. What I'm sayin' is, if you like her and are goin' to treat her with respect, then you're gonna have to be a man about it."

"Okay," he replied not fully understanding what Kieran meant but glad that he somewhat gave him his blessing where Penny was concerned.

⌘

The evening was a lot of fun. They ate Liv's Jambalaya, played dominos, a card game called Spades, which Seth had never heard of but as it turned out was very good at, and laughed most of the night. Charlotte texted Liv around one o'clock letting her know that they would have to pass on coming over. Not long after that, Penny said she was ready to call it a night and they headed out.

Standing on the balcony right outside Penny's door, Seth reached down and wrapped his hand around hers.

"Would you like me to walk you in?"

Pursing her lips into a smile, she replied, "I'm sure Braden's on the couch already so..."

Not wanting the moment to pass him by, he offered, "Would you like to walk me in, then?"

"Sure," with a sweet expression on her face.

Leading her to his door, Seth let go of her hand and unlocked it allowing her to go in first.

Once they were both inside, he closed his door and turned to her. Taking her hand in his again, he lifted it, lightly smiling at her tattoo. Two interlocking hearts, one upside down and the other, right side up.

"Did it hurt?" he asked focusing on the space in the center of both hearts.

Drawing in a slow breath, she whispered, "Yes."

Lifting her wrist higher, he leaned down and carefully touched his lips to the center where there was no ink just bare skin directly in the center of one heart pointing toward him and the other to her.

Seth placed his thumb in the center of her tattoo where his lips had just been as he looked down at her softly sharing, "I can feel your heart beat."

Penny let out a short breath as she closed her eyes tilting her chin up towards him.

Keeping his gentle hold on her wrist with one hand, Seth could feel Penny's pulse quicken as he slowly brushed his fingers against her cheek and down the side of her neck with the other. He moved closer drawing out the moment as long as possible, just in case this was his one and only chance with her and it never happened again. As he watched her lips part in anticipation, Seth closed his eyes and touched his lips to hers.

True to her nature, Penny's lips were warm and sweet as they moved against his. There was comfort in the feel of her smooth skin under his fingertips and the flavor of her lips when he took the opportunity to taste them. She was the cream and sugar that soothed and sweetened all the doubt and anxiety in Seth's otherwise embittered life. And he could only imagine what feeling the rest of her would be like.

Sixteen

Running until his lungs burned, Seth started to wonder how good of an idea it had been to kiss Penny last night. There was no way to gain a better perspective of the situation. It was as if he needed her to breath and there was no way around it. He needed to see her, talk to her, touch her or he would end up suffocating. His run was meaningless, pointless and did nothing to alleviate, it only added to the physical pain he was already in.

⌘

Not knowing exactly what to do with herself, Penny sat in the center of her bed staring at the tattoo on her wrist. Every time she closed her eyes, Seth kissing her was the only thing there. The way his lips felt against hers, the soft touch of his fingers on her skin and in her hair. If kissing him had this kind of effect on her she couldn't help allowing her mind wander to what everything else would be like with him.

Jumping a little when there was a knock at her bedroom door, Penny hopped off of her bed, flung her closet door open.

"Come in," she shouted as she quickly started looking for something to wear.

"You're not ready?" Charlotte fussed, walking into the room.

With an apologetic expression, Penny replied, "Sorry, I don't know where my head is this morning."

"I do," Charlotte assured with a smirk on her face.

Quickly turning away from her closet, Penny exclaimed, "You have no idea! Last night he kissed me and it was, he was... amazing."

"Full body tingles amazing?"

Nodding, Penny swore, "Let's get naked amazing."

Suddenly Braden's voice interrupted them from the living room as he spouted, "Gah, nasty! I can here y'all!" Charlotte made a face and swung Penny's door closed.

Wishing her brother hadn't heard that, Penny flung herself back onto her bed, burying her face in her pillow.

Penny lifted her head saying, "I can't think about anything else."

Seating herself on the edge of Penny's bed, Charlotte asked, "So, no more let's be friends?"

With a heavy sigh, Penny rested the side of her face against her pillow as she looked at Charlotte, pouting, "I don't know."

"Friends with benefits?"

"Ugh..." Penny groaned before reminding, "No sex wagon."

Scowling at her, Charlotte said, "Well then, I say you blow off your plans with me today, get dressed, go knock on his door and see if he's worth a detour on your road to recovery."

"What about bouquet shopping?"

"I'll get Liv to come with me," Charlotte replied before ordering, "Now, put on something cute and go seduce the neighbor."

"That's not..." Penny started to argue before Charlotte stood up saying, "I'm still holding out on your brother so at least one of us should be getting some."

With a disgusted expression, Penny made a gagging sound as she pulled the side of her pillow in front of her face.

Penny heard Charlotte laugh before leaving her room. Why did she insist on bringing up her and Auggie's sex life? Shaking off the general ickiness of that subject, Penny slid off of her bed. Back in front of her closet, she pulled out a sweater and a pair of jeans as she considered Charlotte's suggestion.

⌘

Pacing back and forth in his living room, Seth wanted to go next door and see Penny but was unsure how on the right approach to take. Once he had ruled out kissing her again as a good reason to visit, he'd also decided asking her to a movie was a bad idea. Wishing he had left something of his next door or had something of hers to return, there was a knock at his door.

A heart pounding anxious feeling filled Seth as he walked to his door. Thinking it had to be her, no one else would visit him, he reveled in his nervousness for a moment before opening the door.

The excitement of seeing Penny slowly faded into nausea when he saw his father standing there instead.

"Do you plan on letting me in?" Leonard snapped as Seth stood there staring at him.

"Yes sir, sorry."

Moving to allow his father inside, he had no idea what he was doing there.

After a disapproving scan of Seth's living room, his father stated, "My will has been drawn up and I have been advised to have you sign an acknowledgment form."

"Are you alright?"

Narrowing his eyes at Seth, Leonard assured, "I am perfectly fine. Unlike you, I am invested in this family's future as well as my own."

"Yes sir."

Seth's father opened the folder he was carrying, pulled out a paper that had a red 'sign here' tab, closed the folder and handed it to him with the form on top.

Pulling out a pen from the breast pocket of his suit jacket, he handed it to Seth saying, "I would appreciate it if this did not take all day."

Nodding, Seth took the pen from his father before reading the form header that read, 'Acknowledgment and Agreement of Intent to Disinherit'.

There was a sharp pain in the pit of Seth's stomach as he looked over at his father.

"Is there a problem?" Leonard questioned in a cold manner.

Shaking his head, Seth skimmed down the contents of the page as he heard his own voice slightly crack while replying, "No sir."

It wasn't the fact that he was being disinherited. That had already been clarified by the multiple times Leonard had stated that he disowned him. Seth wanted approval and nothing else from his father, but he couldn't deny how badly it hurt him either. This was intentional and he knew it. His father could have simply stated his wishes in his will. Instead, Leonard was taking the opportunity to remind him of every slight, calloused remark and overall regret of having him as a son he had uttered as far back as Seth could remember.

Seth could feel his breathing pick up as he signed the form and handed it back to his father. Leonard appeared pleased for a moment as he slid it back into the folder, then cringed slightly as he pulled an envelope out.

"Your mother assures me you will be able to rent a tux if you do not have one," he stated handing the envelope to Seth.

As he took the hospital benefit invitation from his father, Seth heard another knock at his door.

"I will let myself out," Leonard shared, heading to the door.

Waiting for the slight relief that would come when his father left, he stared at the wall, this time hoping it wasn't Penny at his door.

A cheery, "Oh, hi! Is Seth home?" followed by a stern, "Excuse me," caused his teeth to clench as the door closed.

"Was that your dad? You look a lot like him."
Nodding, he couldn't bring himself to look at her.

Of all the embarrassing things that had happened since he'd moved in, this was the worst. He didn't want her to see him like this. His breaths were growing shorter by the second, Seth could feel himself repeatedly blinking while shaking his head and it was possible he was going to throw up.

Before he knew what was happening, Penny's arms were wrapped around him.

Pressing her cheek to his chest, she held him tight, soothing, "It's okay."
Seth stood still as his emotions merged from conflicting stages of anxiety to the anxious feel of having her arms around him. Letting out a slow breath, he leaned his head down to rest his chin on the top of her head. When her arms started to loosen from around him, Seth dropped the invitation he was holding and crossed his arms across her back, holding her tight against him. The suffocating distress his father's presence had brought was gone and he could breathe with Penny in his arms.

⌘

Acutely aware that Seth had serious problems with his father that exceeded her own parental issues. Her mom had not spoken to her since Auggie decided to propose to Charlotte. This was obviously a far worse situation. Penny wasn't exactly sure what to do next.

While she was glad to be able to be there for him, she felt like more than a hug was needed at the moment.

Tucked firmly against his chest, Penny asked, "Do you want to talk about it?"

"No," Seth replied before questioning, "Why did you come over?"

A little disappointed by his tone, she replied, "You want me to go?"

She felt him sigh as he answered, "That came out wrong."

"I wanted to see you," she shared giving him an extra squeeze.

As Seth let go of her, she moved back slightly allowing space between them while keeping her arms on his sides.

Smiling down at her, he bit the side of his bottom lip saying, "Me too."

Pursing her lips up into a smile, she could feel excitement radiating through her entire body.

Seventeen

It was getting late in the evening when Seth suggested they sit on the couch and watch a movie. After talking about what he did on a day to day basis at JPT and Penny talked about working at Legacy Ink over turkey sandwiches while sharing a plate at his kitchen table, it was one of those times where you either call it a night or wait to see what will happen next.

While Seth flipped through cable stations looking for a good movie, Penny sat as close as possible to him wondering why he hadn't kissed her yet. She thought for sure he would have earlier but nope, nothing.

"What about this one?"

Glancing at the TV, she wasn't really paying attention to what was on it as she replied, "Sure."

Seth seemed pleasantly surprised as he asked, "You like documentaries?"

Who watches documentaries for fun?

Shrugging a shoulder she said, "I don't think I've ever watched one."

Settling back, he seemed excited as he assured, "I think you will enjoy it. This one is about how ancient civilizations have impacted the modern world."

Oh dear Lord...

Five minutes into the documentary, Penny could feel herself falling asleep. It was hard to believe he thought she would enjoy it? She didn't know whether to be irritated or feel sorry for him. But she did know for sure, a few more minutes of this and she'd be out like a light.

Rolling her eyes as she saw how interested he was in what he was watching, Penny tapped him on the shoulder saying, "Umm, Seth?"

Leaning his head towards her while keeping his eyes focused on the TV, he replied, "This next part is really..." before she cut him off blurting, "Seth."

Turning to her, he had a confused expression on his face.

Tired of waiting for what she had been thinking about all day, Penny scooted up and kissed him.

⌘

There was something about Penny taking the initiative to get things started that nearly drove him out of his mind. Gripping the sides of her sweater Seth pulled her closer as he kissed her back. Feeling her hands slide up the sides of his face to his temples as her fingertips caressed the sides of his head while she deepened their kiss put an incredible strain on his ability to utilize self-control. She was relaxing him and stirring him up all at the same time.

He wanted to say things to her. Tell her how pretty she was, how good it felt to have her so close but when her lips left his, she slid onto his lap and faced him.

"What do you like?" Penny questioned in a soft whisper.

Fighting every instinct, even Seth's brain was screaming 'Now!' as he took her face in his hands.

"This..." Placing a gentle kiss against her lips he shared, "This is what I like."

There was a slight scowl to her expression as if she was trying to figure out what he meant.

"I want more than this moment from you."

Penny glanced down before asking, "How much more?"

Good question.

Scanning the sweet expression on her face, Seth could easily see spending the rest of his life with her. On the other side of his thought was the knowledge that he did nothing for her.

"I think that's one of those things that gets figured out with time."

Her expression was now hesitant as she questioned, "The kind of time where we see other people?"

The thought of Penny being this close to anyone other than him sent a surge of jealousy through him as he replied, "I hope not."

Nodding she shared, "I think this moment just made my all-time top ten."

Her words were inspiring as he offered, "Well, let's see if I can make in the top five."

As she started to laugh, Seth pulled her into a long passionate kiss.

⌘

One last soft kiss from Seth before he said goodnight, made Penny wish they weren't standing at her apartment door. She didn't want the night to end.

Stepping into her apartment, she turned and smiled seeing Seth waiting for her to close her door before he walked back to his door. As soon as she shut the door Penny peered out of her peephole just in time to see Seth bite the corner of his bottom lip as he smiled at her door.

Sighing at his smile and the thought of his kiss, she heard her brother tease, "And what have you been doin'?"

Whipping around to give him a dirty look, she fussed, "Shut up, Braden."

Laughing off her order, he shared, "I think he's a nice guy, Pen."

Shrugging a shoulder at her brother she replied, "I think so too."

Then with a stern look, he advised, "Don't get tired of it, appreciate it."

Penny took a long hard look at Braden before walking over and sitting down on the couch next to him.

"Any idea when I'm going to get my brother back?"

Shaking his head he answered, "I'm the same as I always have been."

Feeling herself tear up she questioned, "Oh yeah? What was the set list tonight?"

Frowning, he looked away, saying, "Things change."

"But some things shouldn't. You're letting her..."

Cutting Penny off, Braden looked at her explaining, "This isn't about Lily. That night she showed up with Keven, maybe he knocked some sense into me when he was beating my ass. 'Cause after that, I was done with her."

"What is it then?"

"It was always the five of us. Then, Will died, Ailin moved and now Auggie's getting married."

Tilting her head to the side Penny stated, "Braden."

Leaning back against the couch, he shared, "I'm happy for Auggie and Charlotte, they're good together."

"But you kinda feel like you're getting left behind," Penny offered starting to understand more what was going on with him.

Nodding, he replied, "Mom's not talking to me either."

Rolling her eyes, she said, "At this point, I don't even know if she's coming to the wedding. She didn't stay mad this long when she found out about Sophia and Ailin."

"I think she's getting crazier the older she gets," he laughed.

Popping him on the arm, Penny laughed too before correcting, "She got over it because Dad was here then."

They both sat silent for a moment.

It was easy for Penny to see where Braden was coming from. His life was getting turned upside down while everyone around him was going on with theirs. Patting his arm she gave an understanding smile as she stood up.

"See you in the morning," she said when it looked like he wanted to be alone with his thoughts.

As she turned to walk away, Penny stopped, hearing him say, "You ever wonder what Liv see's in Kieran."

Taking a deep breath, she turned back to him saying, "No and why are you?"

"I'm just sayin'. Liv's cool as hell and he can be kind of a jerk to her sometimes."

Penny stared at him wondering if he knew about what Kieran had done and whose mark he had.

"Liv's a hand full, you know that and as wild as Kieran was he's always been more laid back."

"Nah, this is somethin' else."

Shaking her head at her brother, she fussed, "If you're starting to have feelings for her because you're lonely or whatever, you need to stop spending so much time with her. She's Kieran's wife."

"I'm not into her like that, it's just..."

Holding her breath Penny worried what he was going to say next.

When he continued to hesitate seemingly unable to find the right words, Penny warned, "You need to leave their relationship to them."

"Alright, Pen. Geez, I was just sayin'," he griped at her as he leaned over and stretched out on the couch.

Shaking her head at her brother, Penny headed to her room.

Changing into her pajama's Penny dwelled on her conversation with Braden for a moment before concentrating on her feelings for Seth. Out of all the guys she had been with, this was the first time she genuinely felt cared for.

Eighteen

A light tapping on her door escalated into a loud knock as Penny woke up hearing her brother shouting at her from the other side.

Jumping out of bed, she stomped over to her door, swung it open and barked at him, "What?"

With a silly sideways grin, he shared, "You got company."

"What?" she repeated, still half asleep.

Laughing at her, Braden turned his head toward the hallway shouting, "You sure you wanna hang out with her? She pretty fricken cranky this morning."

Penny's eyes flew open wide as she lowered her voice questioning, "Seth is here?"

Braden barely had a chance to nod before she slammed the door in his face.

Rushing to her bathroom, Penny brushed her teeth, washed her face and quickly brushed out her hair before hurrying to her closet. Snatching a pair of jeans off of the hanger, she changed into them before grabbing a shirt and pulling it on over her head.

Taking a moment to calm down before she ran into the other room like a damn fool, Penny took a deep breath and ran her fingers through her hair. Although she was so excited she thought she might burst, she didn't want to seem too enthusiastic. Seth always seemed overly cautious. Running up to him and tackling him might scare him away.

Once she felt she had enough control over herself, Penny left her room and walked into the living room.

"Hi," she cheered at Seth as he stood there holding a bouquet of wild roses in his hand.

Smiling down at her, Seth greeted, "Hi, I didn't think you would still be asleep."

"That's okay, are those for me?"

Glancing at the flowers in his hand, he took a step closer and held the flowers out to her.

"Yes."

Penny took the bouquet, making sure to let her hand linger on his before taking it.

With an adoring expression, she looked up at him asking, "Would you like to come into the kitchen with me so I can put these in some water?"

He quietly nodded at her.

Carrying her flowers into the kitchen, she thought this was another top ten moment.

Pulling a large glass pitcher out of the cabinet, Penny filled it with water as she asked, "Did Braden leave?"

"He said he was going to meet Charlotte and Auggie at Kieran's."

Setting the pitcher on the counter, she placed her flowers in it asking, "How did you know these were my favorite? Lucky guess?"

As she turned to face him, Seth replied, "I asked Charlotte when I saw her in the parking lot this morning after my run."

Enamored with the fact that he took the time to ask what she liked, Penny said, "Thank you."

Leaning closer, Seth brushed a few strand of her hair over her ear before placing a soft kiss against her temple.

Closing her eyes, she felt him kiss her cheek and then her chin before making it to her lips. Wanting to press herself against him, she resisted the urge. Penny could tell he was holding back. Sliding her hands into the back of his hair, as soon as she did, he pulled away.

"Would you like to spend the day with me?"

Thinking 'I would like to do all sorts of things with you' she nodded.

With a pleasant smile he questioned, "How do you feel about fish?"

"For lunch?"

Seth's expression was humored as he clarified, "For looking at. There is an aquarium about forty-five minutes away, if you'd like to go."

"Sure, I'll go get my shoes," she replied, shaking off the knowledge that he intentionally stopped their kiss as she walked out of the kitchen.

⌘

Grateful Penny had to leave the room to go get her shoes, Seth needed a minute to collect himself. It was only the two of them in her apartment and the things that were running through his mind the second he kissed her, made his plan of taking things slow with her counterproductive.

On the way to the Sea Center, Penny shared with him how each of her eleven childhood goldfish met their untimely demise. As she talked, he thought about the makeshift pet cemetery in her parent's backyard and was slightly disturbed by her families inability to keep their pets alive.

When they finally made it to the aquarium, Seth stopped in front of a glass wall. Smiling at the calming motion of the brightly colored fish swimming on the other side of it, he used to spend hours just standing there watching them. It was something his therapist had recommended as a way to relax. Standing there with Penny, the fish still had the same calming effect on him as they always had but when Penny slid her hand into his they had nothing on the peace that came with her touching him.

With that thought in mind, he pulled his attention away from the fish and smiled down at her.

"There's a benefit coming up for my grandfather," he started before she cut him off asking, "Is he sick?"

"No, he passed away when I was five. It's a hospital fundraiser that I am invited to."

"Oh, that's right, family of doctors."

Seth cringed at her words for a moment before asking, "Would you like to go with me?"

Penny pursed her lips up into a smile before asking, "Like on a date?"

He wanted to kiss her so badly but, unfortunately, there were kids now running between the rooms.

"Yes, I'm asking you to be my date."

"One condition, you have to be my date to Charlotte and Auggie wedding."

Nodding at her, he replied, "Agreed."

⌘

Feeling like something needed to be said, Penny let go of his hand. Taking a wide step back, she raised her eyebrows and looked up at him.

"So, what are we doing here?"

"At the Sea Center?" he asked with a confused expression on his face.

With a little laugh, Penny shook her head at him.

Understanding reflected in his eyes as he proposed, "Well, an argument can be made for being friends."

"I think we've had that argument."

Seth smiled wide agreeing, "We have," before offering, "We could be more than friends," as they walked into the next room.

The room was dark, barely lit by the glow of the tanks, giving it a private atmosphere and romantic feel.

Slowly turning to face him, Penny questioned, "How much more?"

A serious expression coated Seth's face as he lowered his voice swearing, "As much as you'll let me."

Wishing the group of children that had been running around hadn't just rushed into the room, she quietly replied, "More than friends it is."

Nineteen

Walking up the stairs to her apartment, Penny rolled her wrist around while opening and closing her hand. The tattoo gun wasn't at all like holding a pencil. It felt awkward in her hand and the cord was uncomfortable as it kept brushing against her. It was nothing like she thought it would be; it was hard.

The tattoo skins Kieran gave her to practice on made it even more difficult. Somewhere in her mind she had imagined it to be similar to drawing but in actuality, it was nothing like gliding a sketch pencil across paper. He reminded her several times that it was all about technique and at the end of each day, he'd said she didn't do too bad. But he never once said she did good.

For the last few years, she had been so excited, just imagining the day she would finally get to move beyond set ups and cleaning. Her first week left her with a feeling of frustration and a sore hand. It wasn't like she was going to give up, but she was a bit disheartened. Penny really thought she would be a natural at it.

Hoping Seth would be off over the weekend she hadn't had a chance to see him really since the aquarium. Apparently JPT had acquired a rather large account that was a complete and total mess, causing him to work late every night.

Sliding her key into her apartment door, Penny heard footsteps coming up the stairs. With a bright smile, she turned to see Seth standing on the balcony behind her.

"Busy weekend ahead of you," she commented as she noticed him balancing his briefcase and the stack of files he was carrying.

With a frustrated expression on his face, Seth replied, "You wouldn't believe how messed up this account is."

"Would you like some help?" she questioned as he unsuccessfully tried to shift everything in one arm to get to his keys.

"With the account?"

Shaking her head, Penny stepped closer as a playful smile spread across her face.

Seth continued to appear confused until she slid her hand into the front pocket of his slacks to retrieve his keys for him. Gazing down at her, he bit at the corner of his bottom lip as she slowly withdrew the keys from his pocket.

Thinking if they couldn't spend time together, at least now she would be on his mind, Penny walked to his door unlocked it before opening it for him saying, "Have a great night."

It took Seth a moment to move in her direction.

"You too," he replied as he stepped into his apartment.

Nodding with a smile, she walked back to her door.

Letting out a sigh, Penny turned her key in the doorknob. The week had started out so promising and now even the weekend seemed to be falling flat. As she opened her door, Seth slid in front of her, pulled the door closed and relocked it. Now it was her turn to be confused. Seth held onto her keys while taking her hand as he led her to his apartment.

Penny smiled seeing his briefcase on the floor and the tall stack of files falling over on top of it as Seth closed his door behind them. Tossing her keys next to his, he stepped in front of her. He smoothed his hands down the back of her hair before settling them against the small of her back where the length of her hair ended.

The anticipation was getting hard for Penny to handle as Seth pressed her against him. He definitely had a knack for drawing out a moment.

"My night won't be a great night unless I'm with you." Wrapping her arms around his neck while pushing up on her tip-toes, Penny couldn't wait anymore and kissed him.

How in the world had she gone all week without him? His arms around her with his hands kneading at her sides as his lips moved perfectly against hers. Seth was the right balance of everything.

Hoping this time he wouldn't slow down, Penny unwrapped her arms from around his neck before sliding her hands under his suit jacket and over his shoulders. To her pleasant surprise, Seth let go of her long enough for her to push his jacket down his arms. As his jacket fell to the floor, his hands returned to her sides. Pulling at the knot of his tie, Penny worked at loosening it before his hand covered both of hers.

"I have a lot of work to get finished," Seth shared as he stopped her.

Determined to keep the things going, she offered, "Just consider this a break before you get started," before leading him to the couch by his tie.

⌘

At the moment, Seth couldn't have cared less about the account he was working on or anything else that wasn't her. What he did care about was stopping things before they went too far. It wasn't like she was making it easy for him. In fact, everything having to do with this moment was hard but he was determined to keep a level head and wait for the perfect moment.

The last thing he wanted to do was stop all together but at the same time he was treading a thin line of control over his own body.

Smiling up at him, Penny tugged at his tie as she encouraged, "Come here."

Seth could feel his breathing pickup as he suggested, "Let's go out. Eat dinner."

Penny expression suddenly went from inviting to upset as she let go of his tie and replied, "I'll just go then."

"Wait, no. Don't go," he stressed starting to feel panicked.

He watched her glance off to the side before saying, "Really it's okay. I'm not mad or anything. You have a lot of work to do."

"Penny," he said knowing she was lying to him and urging her to be more honest.

Giving him a half-hearted smile, she replied, "Maybe I'll see you tomorrow," as she stepped away and picked up her keys.

When she walked out of his apartment, the realization of what she was offering and how he turned her down, settled in the pit of Seth's stomach.

It wasn't her fault his mind was getting ahead of her. She more than likely wanted him to be more comfortable so they could spend the evening like they did the other night and he just made it seem like he would rather go to dinner than kiss her. What was wrong with him?

Twenty

Lying in bed only because she refused to get up before seven on a Saturday, Penny tried to think positive. She couldn't understand why Seth was acting this way. Sure it was sweet the first time but now, it was starting to make her feel like he didn't want her. Maybe what they needed were more things in common, shared hobbies and that sort of thing. All of the sudden a burst of inspiration struck her. If he saw her in a more physical light then surely he would want to get more physical with her.

Springing out of bed, she skipped over to her dresser and pulled the bottom drawer open. After digging around, Penny found a pair of grey yoga pants. Quickly changing into them she grabbed a pair of socks and moved to her closet to find a something that at least resembled running shoes.

Posted at her front door, staring out of the peephole, Penny felt a tap on her shoulder.

"Back to stalking are we?"

Rolling her eyes, she glanced at Charlotte before returning to her watch as she replied, "I'm not stalking. I'm waiting."

"Un huh."

"Seth likes to run so I'm going to join him today."

"Oh-kay..."

With a heavy sigh, Penny glanced back to see Braden asleep on the couch before she lowered her voice sharing, "I'm trying to motivate him."

Hoping Charlotte would catch on so she didn't have to say it out loud, Penny raised her eyebrow and nodded.

Charlotte quickly caught on and glanced back at Braden.

Keeping her voice low, she advised, "Stand as close as possible without touching him."

"Why?"

Curling the side of her mouth into a smile Charlotte replied, "It'll make him want to touch you."

"Really?"

"Yea, when a man is attracted to a woman it's his natural reaction."

Nodding at Charlotte's advice, she turned back to the door. Peering through the peephole, Penny saw Seth pass in front of the door.

"Wish me luck," she said before swinging the door open and stepping out onto the balcony.

Noticing Seth had his earbuds in his ears, Penny rushed down the stairs behind him. When he reached the bottom, she quickly made her way around him and waved.

"'Morning!"

An instant smile formed as he removed his earbuds and replied, "Good morning to you."

"Are you going for a run?"

Nodding he looked her over asking, "Are you?"

Pursing her lips up into a smile, Penny shrugged a shoulder saying, "I was thinking about it."

⌘

Seth could feel his chest swell. Knowing that Penny wasn't fond of running but wanted to go with him anyway gave him proud feeling.

Penny had a natural bounce to her walk as they made their way out of the apartment gate and over to the track.

"You need to stretch first," he shared as Penny looked down the track.

"Okay," she replied appearing a bit lost as to what to do next.

She was so adorable with her hair up in a ponytail he didn't want to take his eyes off of her.

Somehow Seth survived Penny stretching in front of him. She appeared awkward and jerky but oh so sexy as she warmed up. It took every bit of his control not to scoop her up and take her behind on of the large oak trees that surrounded the walking path. He tried to focus on stretching and reminding himself of appropriate behavior.

Now, as if things weren't strained enough, she was standing in front of him less than an inch away.

"What now?"

Seth let out a shallow breath as he took a step back.

"Start off slow. I'll keep pace with you."

Taking a step forward, all it would have taken was a deep breath for her to be touching him as she shared, "We don't have to go slow."

Looking down into her sparkling hazel eyes, he replied, "Yes we do."

There was a slight scowl to Penny's expression but her smile remained intact as she nodded at him.

As they started down the path, Seth's legs started to ache. Barely being able to classify what they were doing as jogging, it was more like speed walking. Keeping pace with Penny was starting to make him anxious. His body knew exactly what to do the moment he stepped foot on the track and she was hindering it and him from the exhilarating feel that came with the long strides of actual running.

After trying to speed up a few times and having her fall behind, he was frustrated enough to say something.

"You can pick up the pace a little now."

Glancing at him, she questioned, "I thought we had to go slow?"

Seth found her tone slightly irritating as he replied, "Not so slow it feels like we're running in place."

He could hear the smile in her voice as she asked, "Because you're used to moving faster?"

"Yes, actually."

Her tone was sweet with a hint of underlying sarcasm as she said, "Gosh, that must be really frustrating for you." Seth stopped altogether as he watched her continue at her snail's pace down the path.

Observing her from behind Seth noticed his legs weren't the only part of his body aching now. As an overwhelming feeling set in it occurred to him that Penny might be showing him how he was making her feel. With that thought in mind, Seth took off in a full sprint after her.

Running past Penny, he turned, jogging backwards so he could face her.

"I get it," he shared with a little smile. Taking the opportunity to check her out from the front, as she glanced off to the side and smiled, Seth admired that view also.

"We don't have to go slow anymore?"

With a wide smile he shook his head at her saying, "We can go whatever speed you're comfortable with."

"Okay," she cheered right before she took off running. Seth was surprised and excited, he had to put some effort into catching up with her.

When they made it back to where they started, Penny was hunched over with her hand on her side and her face was bright red.

"Are you alright?" he asked. Taking short gasps of air she nodded.

"Look at me," he said placing one hand on her side and his other hand against her back as he informed, "In through your nose and out through your mouth."

It took her a few minutes of copying his breathing pattern before she finally caught her breath.

Although he was concerned Penny had overdone herself running as fast as she did, breathing in sync with her was an incredible feeling. The soothing calm of their harmonized breathing led his mind to wonder. Seth wished they were no longer standing on the walking path that surrounded the apartment complex. He leaned down to kiss her wanting her inside his apartment underneath the comforter on his bed. Kneading his hand into her side while pressing her against him by the small of her back, Seth drew her into a long slow kiss that escalated with frantic velocity.

Seth's moment of blissful abandonment was cut short as Penny broke their kiss and pulled away.

"No, don't," he instinctively urged needing to feel her against him.

Allowing him to pull her back to him, she leaned her head back saying, "We should head back," as she looked up at him.

He wanted to think they would head back to his apartment to continue what he had just started, but the expression on her face showed otherwise.

⌘

Relieved Seth didn't seem angry with her, when he walked her back to her apartment door and gave her a soft kiss goodbye. After all Penny's 'let's go faster' encouragement, she had stopped him dead in his tracks.

Inside her apartment, Penny saw Charlotte sitting in a chair next to the couch talking to her brother.

"Braden, get out," she demanded needing to talk to her friend.

With a look of shock, he questioned, "Why? What did I do?"

Feeling like there wasn't time to argue, Penny griped, "Just, never mind," before grabbing Charlotte's wrist and pulling her out of her chair.

Practically dragging Charlotte behind her, Penny pulled her into her bedroom and closed the door.

Seating herself on the corner of Penny's bed, Charlotte smiled in anticipation.

"Did my advice motivate him?"

Pacing back and forth, Penny blurted, "No, it didn't."

"Hunh. Well, Seth is kind of an odd guy."

Stopping to face Charlotte, Penny swore, "I should have just stuck to my making friends plan."

Charlotte gave her a curious look before asking, "What happened? I've never seen you like this before."

After taking a deep breath Penny explained, "He kissed me and then he was 'kissing me' and I don't know, I got scared."

"Why?"

"Because, it was... I don't know... It was more than I expected but still not enough and all I could think about was how bad it will hurt in the end."

Sitting back, Charlotte offered, "But what if it doesn't end? What if he's the one?"

Shrugging her shoulders, Penny looked down at the floor.

"Since I've known you I have never seen you get more than a little disappointed over a guy."

"What if he's not?"

Standing up, Charlotte placed her arms around Penny and hugged her imparting, "There's only one way to find out."

Nodding, Penny hugged her back.

Twenty One

Spending the majority of his Saturday going over numbers and trying to make sense of what the previous accountant had done to JPT's newest account's holdings, Seth had to step away. He more than likely would be finished by now if his mind had not kept wandering back to Penny.

Seth sat on his couch flipping through channels trying to think about anything other than her. It was frustrating for her to want him to move faster, then stop him, when he did. He felt uneasy and played with. The only reason he had held back in the first place was because he was trying to show her how much he cared about her. First it was let's be friends then it was I don't want to date you and then she was all over him and did not want to go slow. But now that he wanted to make that leap, she was the one taking a step back. Seriously, what did she want from him?

Riddled with confusion and unable to see how a simple run would satisfy anything after today, Seth had no clue as to what he should do. The thought occurred to him, he should just go talk to her. Penny was pretty upfront about things, if he asked her she would more than likely tell him what her problem was. Feeling comfortable with his decision, he turned his TV off and headed towards the door.

Penny was standing right outside Seth's door when he opened it.

Giving him a sweet smile, she greeted, "Hi."

"Hey... I was just about to," he started to say before she cut him off asking, "Oh, were you going somewhere?"

"I was coming to see you," he answered with a smile before offering, "Do you want to come in?"

Nodding she walked into his apartment with a sudden look of worry in her expression.

Anxiety filled Seth as he hoped she wasn't there to put an end to what was going on between them.

"Umm, I just..." she started at the same time he said, "Look I..."

"Sorry, go ahead," he assured.

Glancing up at him before giving him a nervous smile, Penny shared, "I don't know what this is between us."

Slightly relieved, he replied, "Neither do I."

"Do you, by any chance, know what you want it to be?" Taking a step towards her, Seth placed his hands on her shoulders before sliding them down her arms and taking her hands in his.

"Are you aware that is the most frightening question anyone has ever asked me?"

Penny appeared sad for a moment before covering her expression with a smile as she said, "You don't have to answer."

Apprehensive, it wasn't really a matter of wanting to answer. Seth didn't know if he could answer.

As he looked into Penny's eyes, Seth saw beyond this moment in his apartment, past his need to take things further with her, to a house one day where freshly baked cinnamon rolls sat on the kitchen table. Penny would be smiling at their children, sitting around the table as he wrapped his arms around her and whispered in her ear. Then she would smile up at him and his life would be complete.

Realistically, telling a girl you just started seeing that you could see her having your babies was insane. He couldn't tell her that. She would think he was crazy.

Knowing he had to do something to show her this wasn't something he was taking lightly, Seth remembered the present he bought for her in the home goods section of the local store a few days ago.

Letting go of one of Penny's hands, he held firm to the other saying, "Come see."

Wearing a light smile he could tell she was confused as he led her into his kitchen.

"Close your eyes," he requested before letting go of her other hand.

⌘

Standing in Seth's kitchen with her eyes closed, Penny didn't know why he was trying to show her something in his kitchen. She had put him on the spot. She knew she did. It wasn't necessarily on purpose, however she did want an answer.

Startled when she felt Seth brush his lips against hers, Penny opened her eyes as she looked up at him.

Taking a step back, he informed, "This is for you," as he nudged a package on the counter in her direction.

"You bought me a present?"

Nodding, Seth seemed nervous.

"Can I open it?"

With a slight laugh he replied, "Yes."

Seth's anxiousness made Penny feel a bit apprehensive over what might be inside.

Slowly, she untied the bow before carefully removing the wrapping paper.

"Be careful," he warned as she gave the box a little shake in order to slide the top of the box off.

Unable to imagine what was inside, she hesitated before removing the tissue covering whatever her gift was.

Staring into the box, she heard him ask, "What do you think?" but she couldn't pull her eyes away from the contents inside.

Inside the box sat a black and white polka dotted dinner plate. On top of the plate, there was a matching bowl. A clear tumbler glass stood up from the center of the bowl. Inside the bowl there was a fork, spoon and butter knife tied together by a little yellow ribbon.

She was speechless as Seth reached into the box and pulled out the silver wear. Without a word, he opened his drawer and placed her fork with his before the spoon and then the knife. After closing the drawer, he opened the cabinet. Pulling her glass out, he set it in the cabinet next to his. A warm enthusiastic yearning that started in her toes, rushed through Penny causing her to feel like she was going to blush, as she watched him set her bowl inside his. When he lifted her plate and set it on top of his, she waited for him to close the cabinet door before stepping closer.

The expression on his face showed a concerned curiosity, but that was more than likely because she still had not answered him. The words she wanted to say, she knew were right for the moment but it was far too soon to say them, at least out loud. He was making room for her in his kitchen, incorporating her into his life. It wasn't just a set of dishes he gave her, it was the answer to her question.

Pushing up on her tip-toes, Penny slid her hands up his chest before resting them on the back of his neck.

"Thank you."

Biting the corner of his bottom lip, Seth asked, "You like them?"

Penny's heart grew restless as she tugged him closer whispering, "I love them."

Placing his hands at her sides, he closed the space between them meeting her lips with his.

Swirls of anticipation filled Penny as Seth walked her through the kitchen while continuing to kiss her. She wanted to open her eyes and glance around to see where they were headed, but it quickly turned out to be unnecessary as she heard the sound of a doorknob turning. She felt his bed behind her knees just as he moved his hands to the sides of her face.

Feeling her face grow warm along with the rest of her, Penny grew nervous. This wasn't even close to being her first time but the realization that it could be the first time for something else, caused her to hesitate.

Sliding out of his grasp, she sat down on the edge of his bed.

Seth knelt in front of her, smoothing his hands down the sides of her hair before taking her hands in his, softly assuring, "I'm not in a hurry."

"I just don't want this to end," she shared, needing far too many things from him all at once.

Leaning into her, he rested the side of his head against her shoulder, wrapping his arms around her waist.

"Twelve years of therapy from the time I was seven. Five different therapists. Eight medications. Twenty-three different techniques to alleviate my anxiety. Nothing comes close to you. The way you soothe everything inside of me right down to my soul when I'm with you. I'm not willing to ever give that up."

Unwrapping one of his arms from around her, Seth took her hand and lifted her wrist bringing it to his lips to kissing the center of her double heart tattoo.

Seth's lips made their way from her wrist to the inside of her elbow before he pushed up, pulling both of them onto his bed.

With his hands planted firmly against the bed he hovered over her, swearing, "I don't see an end in my future with you."

His voice was low and deliciously inviting making it hard for Penny to concentrate as she looked up at him, questioning, "You see a future with me?"

Leaning closer, he brushed his lips against hers while saying, "A lifetime of moments like this."

Penny opened her mouth, but the words that were just at the tip of her tongue were now stuck in her throat.

Taking advantage of the moment, Seth deepened his kiss before rolling them both onto their sides. He wrapped an arm around her waist pulling her flush against him.

"You set the pace," he whispered in her ear before nibbling down the side of her neck.

With various emotions coursing through her, an unexpected realization broke through. If he truly wasn't in a hurry, then why was she? She wanted to savor all the moments like this, the ones that would never happen again. When there is still an uncharted mystery in discovering one another. Seth was a man to take her time with.

Before she was lost in the sensation of his lips and his touch, Penny breathed, "I like this."

Dragging his lips across the side of her jaw, he placed a soft kiss on her lips and replied, "Anything you want."

Penny couldn't help but let out a laugh as he smiled and pulled her into another kiss.

Twenty Two

Everything over the next few weeks seemed to flow perfectly into place. Penny's skill had improved enough for Kieran to tell her that her work was looking good. She and Seth had slowly progressed into some serious heavy petting but were still holding out for just the right moment. The wedding was now only two weeks away and although Auggie was unbearable to be around, everyone else, even Braden seemed happy.

Standing in Charlotte's room waiting for her to unveil what she had referred to as the most stunningly beautiful shoes of the face of the earth, Penny shook her head at Liv.

"Wonder if Kieran likes that sorta thing..."

Carefully cutting the box open, Charlotte replied, "My black stilettos are Augustus' favorite. You know sometimes..." before curling the side of her mouth into a smile as she warned, "You might want to cover your ears Penny."

"Maybe you could just not talk about the nasty things you do with my brother."

Laughing, Liv chimed in saying, "We all know Auggs likes to get a little freaky now and then."

As Charlotte started to laugh, Penny glared at them, fussing, "We don't talk about that day, ever."

"All I'm sayin' is Kieran and I've never got butt naked and done it on the kitchen table."

Throwing her hands over her ears, Penny shouted, "Oh Gah, Liv! Shut up!"

Charlotte scolded, "Stop, we did all agree never to bring it up." Just as Penny lowered her hands from her ears, Charlotte added, "Besides he had me bent over it, there's a difference."

"That's it! I don't even want to see your shoes now," Penny griped turning to leave the room.

"No, I'm sorry. We'll stop," Charlotte swore.

With a heavy sigh, Penny replied, "Fine but these better be some spectacular shoes."

"Sorry for teasing but it's only fair," Liv said.

"How is reliving that horrible, horrible day anything but wrong?"

Charlotte answered for her saying, "You're the only one of us getting any right now."

Although slightly grossed out due to the previous subject, Penny knew Charlotte was standing her ground with Auggie but she had assumed Liv and Kieran had worked things out.

Penny stood there silently for a moment before Liv gave her a suspicious look.

"You are, aren't you?"

Charlotte broke in before Penny could answer, questioning, "You haven't slept with him?"

"You say that like it's a crime."

Liv quickly blurted, "She's saying that like she's shocked as hell."

Rolling her eyes at them, Penny shared, "No, we haven't. Yet."

"So what do y'all do?" Charlotte asked.

Trying her best to suppress the smile that instantly formed, Penny replied, "Things."

"Ah, I see," Liv said before asking, "So is he... Skilled?"

"That's really personal," Penny answered in lieu of 'Like you wouldn't believe'.

"I'd say by the shade of red she's turning right now, whatever he's doing makes her one happy Penny," Charlotte enlightened.

Unable to help herself, Penny enthusiastically nodded.

⌘

Leaning back in a chair on Kieran's porch, Seth laughed as he listened to Braden's bachelor party suggestions.

"What if it's a classy strip club?"

Auggie and Kieran shouted, "No!" in unison, shooting down his idea for the fifth time.

"Sor-ry, I was just sayin'..." Braden griped before turning to Seth, asking, "Don't you think..."

Quickly ending that thought, Seth shook his head saying, "There is no way Penny would be okay with that."

Everyone glanced at Auggie for a moment as he made an irritated noise and narrowed his eyes at Seth before shaking his head and looking away.

Cleary he wasn't Cara or whatever anymore. It wasn't like Auggie was real friendly to begin with, but it did seem like he was even less than that since finding out Seth was seeing his sister.

"Ignore him," Braden said before laughing, "He's just extra pissy 'cause Charlotte cut him off until the 'I do's'."

"I can sympathize," Seth replied before Auggie jumped out of his chair and Seth's mind snapped 'You're going to die'.

Auggie lunged at Seth shouting, "What the f..." just as Kieran grabbed him explaining, "Auggs, pretty sure that means they're not."

Seth's chest constricted as he shook his head swearing, "We haven't yet."

"Yet?" Auggie growled at him as Kieran snapped, "Boy!"

Seth's head was warning 'Shut up!-Shut up!' but for some reason he couldn't stop his mouth from saying, "It was my idea not to."

The porch was suddenly completely silent, with the exception of the sound of Seth's breathing.

Kieran stared wide-eyed at Seth and Braden's mouth was hanging open while Auggie gave him a death stare. Trying to judge if he should get up and run or if it was safer not to move, every muscle in Seth body had painfully tensed and he was on the verge of hyperventilating.

"That's my sister," Auggie warned through gritted teeth. Seth frantically nodded at him.

Jerking away from Kieran, Auggie grabbed a Guinness out of the ice chest and sat back down, before Braden leaned over whispering, "Man, I thought you were dead for a minute there."

Trying to regain a sense of composure, Seth barely nodded as he recovered for his near death experience.

Aside from the occasional glare from Auggie, everything had pretty much gone back to normal by the time Penny, Charlotte and Liv pulled up.

Seth watched Penny skip onto the porch before seating herself in his lap. As she kissed his cheek, he quickly glanced at Auggie to make sure his life wasn't in any danger. As it turned out, with Charlotte there she was the main focus of his attention allowing Seth to feel comfortable enough to wrap his arms around Penny.

As Penny sat on his lap smiling, Seth looked around the porch. Braden was closest to him, relaxed and seemingly satisfied to sit there with a beer in his hand. Kieran and Liv were across from them, sitting side by side on the porch swing with his arm around her. Charlotte stood behind Auggie with her arms draped over him as she whispered something in his ear. Auggie's head was tilted towards hers and he had an incredibly anguished expressing on his face. Seth continued staring at them for a moment.

In all honesty, Seth wanted to dislike Auggie. The feeling of 'you will never be good enough' seemed to radiate from him directly to Seth. With that distinct feeling, came a growing need to have his approval. But how do you gain someone's approval when the only reason they disapprove of you is the sole reason you want their approval?

Everyone seemed focused on their own side conversations with the exception of Braden who joined in each of them every time the opportunity presented its self. As it got later in the evening, Penny decided to drive Seth and Braden, back to the Apartment since she rode with Liv and Seth rode with Braden there.

Five minutes into the drive Seth wished they had taken his car to begin with. Braden's El Camino had only one front bench seat and Penny was driving, making it to where Braden sat in the middle between them so Seth had enough leg room. They both had been drinking since early that afternoon and although he really liked Braden, the fact that he kept leaning his head onto Seth's shoulder as he fell asleep was incredibly uncomfortable.

Finally making it back, Seth was relieved to be out of the car. At one point, Braden had leaned so far over he was practically in Seth's lap. Thankfully, Penny's laughter at the situation woke him up enough to where he scooted down a little lower and leaned his head back against the top of the seat.

Inside Penny's apartment, Braden stumbled to the couch and passed out.

Closing the door Penny laughed, "I knew you and Braden were getting to be friends but geez."

Seth leaned his back against the door and smiled, suddenly feeling every beer he had drunk since noon.

"I hate to say goodnight, but I have work in the morning."

"You wanna stay here?" she asked with a hopeful expression.

With a slight laugh, Seth replied, "Your couch is taken."

Penny gave a soft smile before turning and walking out of the living room.

Closing his eyes for a moment, Seth concentrated on what he should do. Slightly inebriated, it was hard for him to distinguish what exactly she was offering. As he glanced at Braden, passed out on the couch, he took a deep breath and pushed off from the door. Heading to Penny's room, whatever the case was Seth wasn't about to turn anything from her down.

Stepping into her room, he looked around. An array of colors surrounded him as he closed her door. From her bright yellow bedspread to her blue dresser there were collages of pictures and drawings covering her walls and multi colored bins that held various art supplies. He instantly felt warmer just standing there. Penny's room was the epitome of her.

Making his way to the other side of her room, to get a better look at her art wall, he focused on a white frame surrounding what looked like old fence posts with Yellow and blue writing that said 'Wake up and be awesome'.

"You like that?" Seth heard Penny ask.

Nodding at her as she stepped out of her bathroom, he replied, "It's very...You."

Wearing the same cupcake pajamas as he had seen her in before, she smiled saying, "I am pretty awesome."

Smiling wide at her, Seth nodded in agreement.

She flashed him a quick smile before skipping to her bed and pulling the comforter back.

As he made his way to the opposite side of the bed, still not knowing what her intentions were, Penny said, "I can set an alarm for you."

"No, I got it," he replied setting his cell phone on the nightstand before asking, "Is it clothing optional."

Hopping onto her bed, she answered, "That's up to you but I know you've had a lot do drink so, I'm not really expecting to do anything but sleep."

Pulling his shirt off over his head, Seth felt a stir of longing for her but was relieved in a way that it would go unsatisfied. At this point, he had come so far with her, Seth felt even if he were in a coma, he would still be up for the occasion. However, when that moment did arrive, he didn't want anything except her in his system.

Seth unbuckled his belt before stepping out of his shoes and slid into her bed, leaving his slacks on the floor. Pulling her to him, he kissed her softly.

"Goodnight," he whispered as she snuggled up to him, tucking her head under his chin.

"'Night."

Closing his eyes, Seth held her close as he realized there was no way he would have the strength to sleep with her without having sex with her first, again.

Twenty Three

Nudged awake out of a dead sleep, Seth rolled over feeling Penny beside him. As he blinked his eyes open, he could hear the alarm on his cell phone but the only thing he cared about was that her smile was what he was waking up to.

"Good morning," she whispered still half asleep.

Reaching behind him, Seth shut his alarm off before wrapping his arm around her and pulling her closer.

"Penny," he breathed as he kissed her forehead.

As she snuggled closer, he kissed her temple before continuing down to her cheek and then the side of her neck.

Somewhere between the feel of her skin under his lips, her body pressing into his and her fingers dipping under the waistband of his boxer briefs, Seth started to lose control of himself.

When the words, "Don't stop," passed through her lips that were brushing against the inside of his shoulder, that was it.

Fully committed to the moment, he tugged at her pajama bottoms with sweet relief being the only thought in his mind.

⌘

Penny pulled back slightly allowing him to remove her top when she heard her doorknob rattle before turning. She quickly jerked the comforter over them before her door swung open.

"Penny Rosin Caffrey!"

Squeezing her eyes shut, Penny tried to wrap her mind around the fact that after months of not speaking to her, Sarah, her mother, decided to pay her a visit at this exact moment.

"You got a tattoo!"

And there it was...

Feeling Seth frozen at her side, she hollered back, "I'll be out in a sec," from under her comforter.

Her mother sounded shocked as she continued to gripe, "Are those men's shoes?"

"Mom! Please! I'll be out in a minute,"

Thankfully, the sound of the door slamming shut was the next thing she heard.

Scowling at the moment and how ridiculous the situation was, Penny felt Seth kiss her cheek.

"Are you okay?"

"I am so sorry," she assured.

Almost in tears as the shock of her mom stopping her and Seth right on the brink of what she had been patiently waiting for the last few weeks, set in.

"I guess I am meeting your mother this morning," Seth said with an encouraging smile.

Throwing her hands over her face, Penny thought 'Why is this happening'.

Unnerved that her mom had taken the liberty of making a pot of coffee in her kitchen, Penny begrudgingly sipped from her cup as she, Seth, Braden and her mom sat around the table.

"What is wrong with you?"

Setting her cup down, Penny replied, "It's not that big of a deal, mom."

Sarah's voice was harsh as she assured, "No respectable man is going to marry you all marked up like..."

"Mom," Penny blurted, knowing she was referring to Liv.

With a look of indifference Sarah stated, "It was Kieran wasn't it. He's appalling."

Giving her mom an 'Are you serious?' look, she replied, "You're his drawer."

Pointing her finger at Penny, Sarah snapped, "That is completely different."

"How is that different?"

Sarah's face started to turn red as she fussed, "Being the marker is a privilege by birthright and he turned into something disgraceful. His father felt the same way. That is why he had an honorable job."

Scowling at her mom, Penny bit her tongue instead of reminding Sarah that her husband was a bartender.

Knowing there was no way to make her mom see how hypocritically outrageous she was being, Penny conceded.

"Okay mom, I'm sorry."

Sarah gave a condescending nod before turning to Braden.

"And what are you doing here?"

With a 'What did I do?' look on his face Braden started to say, "I'm staying here..." before Sarah cut him off griping, "Let me guess, harlot has moved on to you."

"What?" he blurted as Penny snapped, "Mom!"

"I don't hold any ill will against her. I'm just curious how many of my boys she's going to go through before she's satisfied with tainting our family."

Braden gave his mom a nervous smile as he assured, "Charlotte's still with Auggie mom. The wedding's next Saturday."

Appearing insulted, Sarah looked away from Braden and directly at Seth.

Penny watched as her mom seemed to be mentally scrutinizing him.

With a slight nod, Seth introduced himself saying, "Seth, Mrs. Caffrey."

"Can I assume you are between jobs? Some sort of artist? Low life musician?"

Penny shook her head in disbelief at the lengths of her mom's hypocrisy as Braden gave his mom a 'Gee thanks' look.

"No ma'am, I'm an accountant at JPT Financial."

Sarah stared at him for a moment before her whole face lit up.

"You're Jackson's Seth?"

Giving her a strange look, he replied, "He is my boss."

Grabbing hold of the crucifix around her neck, Sarah said, "After all this time, my prayers are finally answered."

Placing her forehead in the palm of her hand, Penny shook her head.

Penny heard Seth's chair scoot back before he said, "Well, it was nice to meet you. I had better go get ready for work."

"Oh, the pleasure is all mine, Seth," she assured before fussing, "Penny, go walk him out."

Rolling her eyes, Penny stood saying, "Yes ma'am."

Following Seth to the door, Penny thought 'It will be a miracle if he doesn't pick up and move after this'.

Ready to apologize for what he just had to endure, Penny was a little confused to see Seth unsuccessfully repressing a smile.

"You think this is funny?" she questioned in a quiet voice.

Giving her a quick kiss, he replied, "I think I am going to be late for work if I don't go get ready."

Nodding Penny opened the door, receiving another goodbye kiss before he walked out.

After closing the door behind him, Penny walked back into the kitchen.

Instantly stressing her approval, Sarah shared, "You know, there are quite a few family names that would be perfect for your children," as Penny sat down at the table.

Leaning over and placing her forehead against the table Penny covered her head with her arms thinking, 'Why?' as Braden started to laugh.

⌘

The day was moving along quickly for Seth. With four active accounts and three pending for his team, he was more than happy to be buried in paperwork. The faster the day went by, the sooner he would get to go home and see Penny.

Walking into Jackson's office, carrying the quarterly reports, Seth had worked himself down to only an hour left. Placing the files on his boss's desk, he watched Jackson motion for him to have a seat while talking on the phone.

Feeling a tiny bit restless, Seth was anxious to get back to his desk and finish out the day.

Shaking his head with a wide smile, Jackson said, "Apparently Sarah has taken a liking to you."

"She seems like an older, meaner version of Penny," he replied without thinking before apologizing, "I'm sorry I didn't..."

Jackson cut him off laughing, "Ren will love that one," before he assured, "Don't worry about it."

"Yes sir," he replied feeling uncomfortable now for just having insulted a member of his family.

Leaning forward, Jackson placed his elbows on top of his desk before folding his hands together informing, "I have been meaning to have a conversation with you for a while now."

Nodding, Seth started to feel uneasy.

"When the Temp Agency sent you here six years ago, I honestly didn't think you would last more than a week or two. But you did. Over the years, I've watched you strive, not toward success, to become your own man."

Seth stood as he watched Jackson push away from his desk before walking over to him.

"Now, I realize I'm overstepping my bounds here but since you are seeing Penny and she's my family, I'm taking the liberty anyway."

There was a hesitation before Seth questioned, "Sir?" not knowing what he was about to say.

Placing his hand on the back of Seth's shoulder, Jackson shook his hand, imparting, "I'm sorry your family doesn't see the man you are. I do though and I am proud of you."

Seth felt his jaw immediately lock, unable to respond.

With an extra pat on the back, Jackson smiled wide at him saying, "Now get back to work so I can give you Friday off for Auggie's bachelor party."

All Seth could do was clench his teeth and nod, finding it hard to process the emotion of having someone he looked up to be proud of him.

⌘

Taking her time to finish one more outline, Penny would be moving on to shading after this particular one. The swirls of the mermaid tail were actually a piece of cake compared to the short straight lines that made the scale pattern.

It was a little strange to her that Kieran was making her practice a mermaid, she had never seen one tattooed on someone before, and she had seen a lot of tattoos since working there. But Kieran was all about tradition and he said his dad told him when he started, that you have to master all your basic skills in order to create a flawless one.

As she worked on it, Liv leaned over her shoulder.

"You should give her some personality. Have her smirk and give Kieran the finger," she suggested with a laugh.

Penny let out a laugh of her own, saying, "That'd be funny."

Faintly hearing the bell above the shop door ring, Penny glanced in that direction.

Liv whistled before saying, "Look at Miss Society here."

Walking over to them Charlotte replied, "Bridal shower brunch my ass, it was more like Be a B Day for every snotty woman in this town."

Penny gave her a compassionate expression before noticing Charlotte raise her eyebrows and Liv nod back at her.

Curious, but invested in finishing her mermaid, Penny leaned her head down and focused on the tattoo.

Kieran stepped out of the back saying, "Hey Charlotte, what brings you by?"

Before Charlotte could answer, Liv said, "I'm ready to go."

Without looking up, Penny could tell Liv and Charlotte were up to something.

"As soon as Pen's done," he assured before Liv said, "Charlotte's here and Penny can lock up. Come on, I'm starving."

There was silence for a moment before Charlotte confirmed, "I'll lock the door behind y'all. We'll be fine."

Hesitantly, Kieran agreed before warning, "Alright but no one else needs to be here after hours."

Penny could hear the smile in Charlotte's voice as she swore, "Just me and Penny."

"Come on," Liv demanded before Charlotte walked them to the door.

Once the shop was locked up with Penny and Charlotte inside, Charlotte pulled a chair up next to her.

Finishing her last few lines, Penny asked, "What's up?"

"You are my best friend, Penny."

"I'm also your roommate, maid of honor and soon to be sister in law."

"I know, that's why I'm coming to you."

Finished with the last line, Penny set her gun in its clip next to her table saying, "Please don't tell me you're having second thoughts."

"What? Of course not."

Twisting her chair towards Charlotte, Penny gave her a suspicious look.

"I know what I want to get Auggie for a wedding present."

"Marrying him isn't enough?"

Scooting closer Charlotte shared, "It's not really a gift. It's more like a declaration."

"And..."

"And I can't do it without you."

Shaking her head with a smile, Penny said, "Okay, what do you want."

"A tattoo."

Stunned, Penny replied, "Oh no."

"Please, it's nothing big."

"Charlotte I can't. I'm not ready. Why don't you just have Kieran do it?"

Appearing to get irritated with Penny, Charlotte shared, "For one, the location of it," as Penny made a face she continued, "Really though, I want it to be a secret."

"Then get him to do it, it's not like he hasn't seen a ton of girls naked before and besides he's like a vault, he won't tell."

"Yea, I wouldn't be so sure of that," Charlotte muttered.

"What do you mean?"

With a loud huff, Charlotte replied, "Nothing, it doesn't matter. The point is, I want you to do it."

Shaking her head, Penny scowled at her persuasiveness.

Charlotte narrowed her eyes at Penny and then smiled.

"Penny, I trust you. Please. It would be an honor to be your first tattoo."

With a heavy sigh, Penny could no longer fight against Charlotte's coercion or her own curiosity over what it would be like to tattoo actual skin.

Taking a deep breath, Penny replied, "What do you want and where do you want it."

Twenty Four

With Braden at Kieran and Liv's for beer and pizza night and Charlotte having a girls night with her mom and sisters, Penny decided to make up for the other morning with Seth by cooking him dinner.

She had just finished setting the table when there was a knock at her door. Skipping to answer it, she was anxious to see where the night would lead. The last few days Seth had seemed a bit skittish around her. Penny knew her mom was a lot to take in, especially when she was mad, but she was hoping it was more because of how close they came to sealing the deal.

Opening her door with a cheery smile, she let Seth in as she eyed a package in his hand.

"You're early."

"I know, sorry, do you want me to come back later?"
Feeling like something was wrong she let him in, hoping she was just being silly.

"I hope you like roast, it's not quite ready though," Penny shared as she turned to head back towards the kitchen.

Seth followed her complimenting, "It smells good."

As soon as they reached the kitchen, she couldn't stand it anymore, asking, "What's in the box?"

"Dessert."
Thinking that was sort of a vague answer, Penny nodded.

Opening the refrigerator, she pulled out a tray of cheese cubes and set them on the counter.

"Do you want something to drink?"

"No, thank you."

"Is something wrong?"

"No."

Penny could feel her heart starting to sink, it didn't matter what he said, he showed all the warning signs of 'I'm going to break up with you'.

⌘

Anxious, Seth wished he had waited the extra hour to come over. He was trying to be cool about it but every time he looked at her, he recalled the other morning before her mother interrupted them. It was getting to be unbearable.

Glancing down at his shoes, he tried to think of anything and everything that had nothing to do with them being in her apartment alone.

"About how long until it's ready?"

Her voice sounded sad as she replied, "Should be around forty-five minutes."

Drawing in a breath before letting it out, he nodded.

"You don't have to sit around and wait for dinner. If you have something to say, just say it," she suddenly snapped at him.

Caught off guard by her tone, Seth stared at her for a moment.

He tried to look away and get some kind of handle on the moment but couldn't. He felt desperate. Anguished even and the longer he looked at her, the worse it got.

"I want you," he swore not even sure at first if he had said it out loud or not.

Then, by the stunned expression on Penny's face he knew that he had.

It was hard to distinguish who moved first, it was possible they had leapt at each other at the exact same time but it didn't matter at all. All that mattered was that Penny was in his arms, pulling at his belt buckle while unbuttoning his shirt as she kissed him back.

Trying to keep a level head while going out of his mind, Seth broke their kiss.

"Should we go to your room?"

Penny, pulled his lips back to hers before kissing down his neck.

"Yes."

Every nerve in Seth's body was on high alert as they made their way to her room, leaving a trail of clothes behind them.

Crashing down onto her bed, he wrapped his arms around her tight as he rolled her on top of him. Caught up in the best anticipation of his entire life, Seth smoothed his hands down her bare sides before spreading them across her behind as he pressed her against himself.

Savoring each invigorating movement, that was without a doubt leading to a higher state of elation, lead Seth to a moment of clarity.

Rolling Penny onto her back, he leaned over her saying, "I need to..." before she stopped him assuring, "Sit back, I've got it."

Sliding to the head of the bed, he sat there watching her as she reached down and pulled his wallet from his slacks.

Sitting in front of him, Penny's eyes trailed the length of him before softly asking, "May I?" as she tore the condom wrapper open.

Seth slowly nodded before leaning his head back against the wall as he closed his eyes.

After using every ounce of willpower he had to stay focused and not give in to the sensation of her touch, Seth took a calming breath and opened his eyes. A smile of anticipation formed on her lips as she sat between his legs facing him. Her hair flowed around them, brushing against the tops of his thighs as she leaned forward and gently kissed his lips. Allowing himself one more controlled breath, Seth smoothed her hair back over her shoulders so he could take in all of her beauty before trailing his fingers down her sides and grasping her hips with his hands. Lifting her onto his lap, he watched Penny's eyes flutter closed as she leaned her head back letting out a blissful sigh. Sliding his hand to the side of her face while she slowly rocked forward, Seth found an inner peace there inside of her he never knew existed.

⌘

Dazed from a moment that exceeded every expectation Penny had for her and Seth together, she rested her cheek against the inside of his shoulder. His arms were wrapped securely around her while his lips grazed her forehead in between breaths.

There were no words that could describe the way he had moved her, inside and out just moments ago or how she was feeling now.

A light smile found its way to her expression when she heard him softly ask, "Are you falling asleep?"

"Do you need to get up?"

Reluctantly moving off of him when he replied, "Yes," Penny watched him slide out of bed and grab his underwear off of the floor on his way to the bathroom.

"You have a cute butt," she blurted, earning her a wide over the shoulder smile, just before he stepped in and closed the door.

With a happy sigh, Penny snuggled down into her comforter as she waited for him to come out.

Smiling at the bathroom door, an unpleasant thought made its way through her happiness. Would he come out, get dress and go home? What about tomorrow? Was he still going to want her as much as he did before? Feeling herself scowl, Penny didn't want to think in those terms. Wanting to revel in the moment and enjoy it, these were concerns she had never had before.

When Seth came out, Penny was lying on her back staring at the ceiling.

"Is everything alright?" he questioned stepping to the side of her bed.

Glancing up at him, she nodded before scooting over.

As he slid in bed next to her, he wrapped an arm around her asking, "Are you sure?"

"I'm falling in love with you," Penny shared, needing some reassurance that what was between them was going to last.

She could feel the smile on his face as he nuzzled into the side of her neck.

"That's good to hear since I've already fallen in love with you."

Pulling back slightly, Penny smiled, "You have?"

Nodding with a serious expression on his face, Seth swore, "I love you."

Penny's heart was full in every way possible now as she replied, "I don't know what to say."

Seth appeared confused before saying, "I think that I love you too would be a nice response."

"Oh, I do! I love you too," Penny cheered at him.

Happily satisfied, he leaned in to kiss her then stopped half way, questioning, "How much longer until the roast is done?"

Glancing at her alarm clock Penny replied, "Around five minutes."

"Challenge accepted," he stated as he pulled her against him.

Twenty Five

Feeling the comforter move down her side, Penny opened her eyes just in time to see Seth sliding out of bed. Laying still, she closed her eyes so he would think she was asleep. She didn't want him to leave but at the same time, Penny wanted to know what he wanted.

The moment Penny heard a door close she opened her eyes. With a heavy sigh, she drug herself out of bed. Skipping out before she woke up didn't exactly feel like an 'I'm in love with you' move but then again maybe he just needed to get something and planned on being back before she woke. Stepping into her bathroom, she decided to shake Seth leaving off and start her day.

After her shower, Penny wrapped a towel around herself before stepping back into her room to get dressed.

Startled a bit, to see Seth sitting on the edge of her bed, she blurted, "Oh, hi. I thought you left."

Shaking his head, he replied, "I was in the kitchen."

"Are you hungry?"

A weary smile spread across his face as she stepped closer to him.

"I made a pot of coffee."

"That was nice of you," she replied, feeling the moment turn awkward.

⌘

Watching her turn and head to her dresser instead of to him, Seth started to feel nervous.

"You're welcome," he replied, feeling like he had overstayed his welcome.

Tilting his head to the side, he stared at the floor as she got dressed.

Mentally chastising himself for being so open and honest with her last night, he'd said some things that more than likely could have waited. On top of telling her that he was in love with her after he made love to her, he had opened up to her and shared how he could see the family he had always wanted in her. At the time, her smile beamed, and she had even blushed a little showing him she liked the sound of what he was saying. Maybe now, the next morning, it was too much to take in and she was having second thoughts. And who could blame her. Penny had plans for her life. He knew how important becoming a tattoo artist was to her. It was amazing to him that she was making it happen for herself. However, last night while eating the roast that she cooked, after having made love to her twice, all he could think about was having her bake and have babies for him. 'I am such a jackass' he thought, disappointed in himself.

Sitting at Penny's kitchen table, Seth stared down into his cup of coffee, not knowing what to say to her. She was quiet which made it even harder for him each time he thought of breaking the silence.

Deciding he just needed to get out of there and give her time to think about things, Seth looked up at her sharing, "I should go."

Without looking at him, Penny shrugged a shoulder at him saying, "If that's what you want."

He started to stand up then changed his mind turning his body towards her.

"Penny."

"Yea?" she replied still not looking at him.

Frustrated, he questioned, "Why are you acting this way?"

After receiving yet another shoulder shrug from her, Seth stood up and started to leave.

Before making it out of the kitchen, Seth changed his mind.

"You're something else, you know that."

Sitting straight up in her chair, Penny turned giving him a confused glare.

"You shouldn't say things you don't mean."

Hopping, up she fussed, "Well, neither should you," back at him.

Seth wanted to tell her off for giving him the cold shoulder and then trying to put it off on him like he had done something wrong. But as he looked at her, all he could see was the worried look in her eyes behind her irritated expression.

Swiftly walking up to her, he leaned his head down toward hers, looking her directly in the eyes.

Keeping his tone soft while remaining serious, he assured, "I don't say things I don't mean."

"Neither do I," she insisted.

Placing his hands on her shoulders, he admitted, "I'm so confused right now."

A smile broke through Penny's argumentative mood and she started to laugh.

Shaking his head, Seth asked, "Why are you laughing?"

Throwing her arms around his neck, she answered, "This is so absurd, I can't help it."

Trying to make sense of her, Seth questioned, "You're not having second thoughts about us?"

Penny shook her head at him before letting her hands slide down the front of his shirt as she took a step back.

"This isn't a conversation for the kitchen," Penny informed before motioning for him to follow.

A hint of excitement was building when the idea that it might be one for the bedroom entered his mind.

Following her into the living room, Seth was once again confused when instead of heading to her room, Penny walked to the front door.

"Do you have your keys?"

Patting the side of his pants pocket, he nodded.

Opening her door, Penny stepped out on the balcony as she said, "Close it, please."

Seth closed her apartment door before following her to his.

"Why are we..." he started to question, stopping when her hand slid into his slacks to retrieve his keys from his pocket.

Penny unlocked his door and opened it.

Drawing in a deep breath, Seth closed his apartment door behind himself. He stood in his living room for a moment watching her disappear into the hall that led to his bedroom. Wondering what sort of secret conversation she wanted to have that they could discuss in his bedroom, he was curious and honestly a little concerned. Did she want him out of her apartment so she could quickly leave if necessary or was it simply a change of scenery?

Penny was standing in his room next to his bed with a sweet smile on her face. As he made his way closer she sat down.

Taking a seat next to her on his bed, Seth informed, "Am I supposed to understand what's going on here? Because, I don't."

"Charlotte or Braden could be back any minute and I didn't want them to interrupt us."

Even though that was understandable Seth was still very confused.

"Were you serious about everything you said last night?"

"Yes."

Tilting her head to the side in a compassionate manner, she pressed, "Are you sure because it really is okay if you were just caught up in the moment."

Slightly insulted, Seth replied, "That's offensive."

Almost pouting, she scowled, "How is that offensive?"

"You're basically calling me a liar."

Appearing as though she didn't understand his point of view, Penny replied, "No, I'm giving you an out in case you didn't really mean it."

"When people say things they don't mean, it's called lying."

Glancing off to the side she had a perplexed look on her face like she couldn't put the two together.

"Penny, I promise you, I do not say things unless I mean them."

Pursing her lips up into a smile, she nodded her approval.

Twenty Six

Standing in between Charlotte and Liv, Penny stared into the full-length mirror at the champagne gold, floor length gown she was wearing in the fitting room of La Bella Couture.

"I like it," Penny said before adding, "It's just a lot fancier than what I'm used to."

Giving her a pat on the shoulder, Charlotte informed, "The benefit is black tie."

With a worried expression, Penny shared, "I'm going to feel so out of place there."

"Emerson and Amila are going. Oh, and Silvia will be there too."

Making a face at Charlotte in the mirror, Penny asked, "Silvia?"

Laughing, Charlotte replied, "Awe, but she's always so nice to you."

"I know she's your sister but if I have to hear how hot my brother is one more time, I just might throw up on her."
Continuing to laugh, Charlotte teased Penny, reciting Silvia's comments to her while they were being fitted for their bridesmaids dresses a few weeks ago.

"Oh my gosh Penny, Braden is like so... Mmm. He's like so incredibly hot!"

As Penny wrinkled he nose and shook her head at Charlotte, Liv said, "I think he is."
Both Penny and Charlotte leaned their heads toward Liv in surprise.

"What?" Liv blurted.

"I'm going to pretend you never said that," Penny shared as she stepped back behind the dressing room curtain.

Unzipping the gown, Penny could hear Charlotte and Liv, even though they had lowered their voices. At first she tried to ignore them, then her concern got the best of her and she couldn't help herself.

"Really? You think Braden's hot?"

"Don't you?"

"He's a good looking guy but its Braden."

Pulling her jeans back on, there was silence for a moment.

"Have things gotten better between you and Kieran?"

"No."

"I don't understand what his problem is."

"You?"

"Is it still about Braden's tattoo?"

"I don't know anymore. It's been almost six months."

"Y'all haven't had sex in six months?"

"A few weeks ago we almost did."

"Liv..."

"It's cool though, hopefully what I'm wearing to your wedding will do the trick."

"If he's anything at all like Augustus, those heels you got will make him rise to the occasion."

"Hope so, 'cause at this point it's all I can do not too dry hump his leg, I want it so bad."

Hearing them laugh, Penny stepped out from behind the curtain.

Penny held up her gown with a smile on her face. It was hard for her hear what Liv was saying because she loved them both and wanted her and Kieran to be happy. It did seem as though Liv had a plan, and although she thought it was unfair of Kieran to be punishing Liv for something he caused, Penny knew everything would work out between them.

⌘

Driving out to Kieran's house, Seth could feel Braden staring at him from the passenger seat.

Trying to break the uncomfortable tension that was taking over their car ride, Seth asked, "Are the girls meeting us out there later."

"That's what I heard."

"You have something you want to say?"

"That depends."

With a heavy sigh, Seth questioned, "Is this about me and Penny?"

He could hear the strain in Braden's voice as he replied, "Nah, you're good for her. It's about Liv."

"Liv?"

"Don't get me wrong I'm not into her like that. She's Kieran's wife. It's just... Man, I don't know."

Nodding, Seth said, "I don't know if I'm the right person to talk to about this."

"Are you gonna say somethin'?"

"No."

"Then you're the right person."

Realizing Braden needed someone to talk to, Seth offered, "Alright, I can't promise you good advice but I'll listen."

Braden nodded, then turned, looking out the passenger window.

It took several minutes before Braden started talking.

"The first time I met Liv, Kieran brought her to a party I was playing at. She had this smirk on her face like she knew something I didn't and when Kieran introduced us, she called me a punk, shook her head and walked off."

Seth couldn't help laughing as he thought from the short time he'd known Liv, it sounded just like her.

"It took her a while to warm up to me. Which was weird 'cause most people like me right of the bat, I'm a likable guy."

"Not to rush your story but we're almost there."

"Anyways, last night we were playing a board game and Liv beat the pants off me and Kieran. She was doing her standard, I kicked your ass dance because she never loses, and he made her go to bed."

"And that bothered you."

"It pissed me off."

"Why?"

"I like hanging out with her."

Seth thought for a moment before asking, "Are you jealous that he gets to go to bed with her and you don't?"

There was a long pause before Braden replied, "I think so, not 'cause I wanna go to bed with her though. She's cool as hell and he's always trying to put her in check. He doesn't appreciate how awesome she is."

"So you're looking at this from a friendship perspective?"

"Yea."

"Alright, I think I understand now. You're mad because Kieran has someone like Liv and you don't."

"That's it!" Braden snapped his fingers, sitting straight up in the passenger seat before adding, "Man, you are really good at this."

Not so sure about that but pleased to have helped Braden out, Seth pulled up to Kieran's house.

⌘

After dinner and a full day of shopping, Penny was happy to give the passenger seat to Liv and sit in the back seat of Charlotte's car. She listened to them in the front seat for a while. Liv was saying how lame it was to hang out with the guys for her bachelorette party while Charlotte insisted she would rather spend the evening with her friends and soon to be husband than to do anything else.

It wasn't long before Penny's own thoughts took over drowning out their voices. She'd been in a lot of relationships, if you could really call them that. No one had come close to saying the things Seth said to her. His words were something she had waited her whole life to hear but the more she thought about his declarations, the more her concern over them grew. It wasn't like she didn't believe he meant them, she just wasn't sure that he always would. The fact that he had already said them and how they made her feel, told her this was something chocolate and peanut butter wouldn't fix when he changed his mind.

Feeling herself actually start to frown as she fretted over the situation, Penny thought about the look in his eyes when Seth said he was in love with her and started to smile.

"Whatcha thinkin' about back there, beautiful?"

Charlotte answered, "Her lover," in a teasing tone.

With a loud laugh, Penny replied, "Oh dear lord."

Adjusting to look at her, Liv asked, "So Lurker's the one, huh?"

"He says he is."

Glancing at Penny through the rearview mirror, Charlotte blurted, "What?"

Noticing the equally crazy look Liv was giving her, Penny corrected herself saying, "The things he says makes me think he might be."

In unison, they asked, "Like what?"

"He said he doesn't see an end to his future with me."

"Damn Penny, that's," Liv started to say before griping, "What the hell?" as they turned onto her gravel driveway. Penny scooted forward, looking out the windshield of Charlotte's car.

Stopping halfway down the driveway, Charlotte parked her car as Liv swung the passenger door open and leaped out.

"Why is my couch in the middle of the yard?" Liv yelled before hollering, "Is that our mattress?"

As Penny slowly got out of the car, she heard Kieran's voice in the distance inform, "You said you wanted a new one and it's the bed out of the spare room."

Taking in the scene, there wasn't just a couch and a mattress in the yard. There was what looked like a two ladders covered with a tarp and another one strung between two trees. Tires, a tractor and all the chairs from the porch were scattered throughout the yard. Shaking her head, Penny could help but smile.

As she followed Charlotte and Liv up the driveway, Penny was quickly lifted off of her feet.

Before she could register what was happening she heard Seth shout, "I've got a hostage," as he flung her over his shoulder and ran behind the tarp between the two trees.

"She's not a hostage if you're the only one that wants her," Braden shouted, prompting her to gripe, "Gee thanks," in response.

Seth put his finger to his lips and then peeked around the tree.

There was a paintball splatter that just missed his head hitting the tree instead just before they heard a loud pop and Charlotte shout, "Augustus Caffrey!"

The sound of footsteps running through the yard was next before Liv informed, "I got Auggs' spot."

"That was close," Seth whispered, pulling Penny down to crouch behind the tree with him.

There were a few more popping sounds in the distance, then silence.

Appearing cautious, Seth peered through the space between the tarp and the tree.

"Are you having fun?" Penny asked in a quiet voice.

"Fun? We are at war," he whispered back.

Penny placed her hand over her mouth, retraining a laugh.

"You might want to surrender now that Liv's playing," she suggested in a hushed tone.

When he turned back to look at her, Liv pressed her paintball gun to the side his head saying, "Because I don't lose. Now hand it over."

Handing his gun over, Seth looked at Penny as she smiled an 'I told you so' smile.

Sliding his gun in the back of her pants, Liv asked, "Alright Lurker, where do you want it?"

Breathing out a heavy sigh while curling his arm into his chest, Seth turned his shoulder towards her.

Wincing as soon as the paint splattered against the arm of his shirt, he shouted, "Man down."

Liv winked before silently stepping away.

⌘

The stinging sensation where Liv shot him was replaced by an altogether different one as soon as Penny started to unbutton his shirt.

Keeping his voice low, he asked, "What are you doing?"

Rolling her eyes at him, she replied, "I'm going to check out your arm. You're going to have a huge bruise."

Even though he had an undershirt on, it felt like she was undressing him.

Stopping her hand right before she reached the last button, Seth leaned closer whispering, "Will you stay at my place tonight?"

Nodding, Penny leaned in and kissed him.

Three loud pops and Braden hollering, "Damn Liv! Alright! Ya got me," interrupted their moment.

Looking at each other, they started to laugh. This was definitely the best bachelor party he had ever been to.

Twenty Seven

Lying in Seth's bed, Penny held back a giggle as Seth stretched her leg high in the air and placed a soft kiss behind her knee.

"And definitely, this spot," he assured before lowering her leg and placing another kiss on her side right above her hip.

After an amazing round of morning sex, Seth was making a point to show her every part of her body that turned him on.

Penny's head swam with delight as she said, "You're determined to replace every single one of my top ten aren't you."

Sliding up eye level with her, Seth smiled sharing, "I'm really hoping to get all around favorite."

Running her fingers into his hair, she sighed, "That's a tall order."

"I am a tall guy," he replied, pulling her all the way against him.

Penny smiled wide at his odd sense of humor as she wrapped and arm and a leg around him.

Seth nuzzled into the side of her neck, hooking his arm under hers and around her back.

His voice was low and serious as he questioned, "Do I make you feel good?"

An involuntary gasp escaped her. It was the sweetest, sexiest most loving thing anyone had ever asked her.

"Like no one else," she softly replied in his ear.

As he held her tighter, she almost said I love you but held her tongue since neither of them had said it again since the first time.

⌘

Pacing back and forth in his living room, in front of his coffee table, every time Seth would glance at the hospital benefit invitation his chest would constrict. Why was he going and why did he ask Penny to come with him? Being with her was like a dream so what made him think involving her in this nightmare was a good idea. Clearly he wasn't thinking. Spending the last few weeks in his Penny bubble, must have given him a false sense of security.

He was starting to feel sick, visualizing the different possible scenarios of how the evening ahead could play out. The least unpleasant would be the one where they were flat out ignored. The thought eased Seth's mind as he considered, no one would want to talk to them anyway. He was definitely okay with that. In fact, being ignored would be wonderful. They would just keep to themselves and be back under his comforter in no time.

Standing outside Penny's apartment door, Seth checked the inside breast pocket of his Tux one last time to make sure he had his invitation. Looking forward to the calming feeling that would come as soon as she was standing next to him and he could touch her, Seth knocked on her door.

The door slowly opened and Seth was speechless. Penny was always so pretty but tonight she was beauty beyond words. Her long auburn hair was pulled into some sort of an up-do leaving her shoulders completely bare in her gold strapless gown.

"We don't have to go," Seth managed to say feeling like she was an angel and he was bringing her to the demon court.

Giving him a strange look, Penny asked, "Is that your way of saying I look nice?"

Seth nodded, but it was a lie. What he was really saying was, 'Your too sweet and beautiful to be subjected to my family, introduced to Satan, otherwise known as my father, or his mistress, my mother'.

As Penny and Seth walked into the banquet hall, he reached down to take her hand.

Hooking her arm around his instead, she shared, "Charlotte gave me some tips for tonight."

Wanting the security of her hand in his, he replied, "That's good," without feeling good at all about it.

Suddenly stiff the moment he spotted his father, Seth purposely led Penny in the opposite direction. Unfortunately, hoping to find comfort in a crowd of strangers, he mistakenly led them straight to his grandmother.

Seth watched his grandmother's overly superior expression fall on him before scrutinizing his date.

"Grandmother," he greeted with a short nod.

"I appreciate you joining us this evening," she replied before chiding, "I am aware this is not your circle of people," as she turned her nose up at Penny.

Instinctively, he tightened his arm around Penny's before turning and walking in the other direction.

As Seth headed to the open bar on the other side of the room, he felt her stroking the top of his arm. There was a light sting from the bruise Liv left on him, but it was also a reminder of the vast difference between her family and his.

He looked down at her sparkling hazel eyes just in time to hear her comfort, "It's okay, my Nana is kinda mean too." It wasn't okay, not in the slightest, but her attempt to make light of his grandmother's rudeness made him smile anyway.

They were almost to the bar when Seth heard a squeal and Penny's name, loud enough that everyone around them turned around.

A young brunette wearing a hot pink sparkly dress and way too much mascara practically ripped Penny away from him as she blurted, "Oh my gosh! You look amazing!"

There was a pleasant expression on Penny's face as she greeted, "Hi Silvia."

"Charlotte said you were coming. Mom and daddy are just over there," she announced, pointing behind them before waving her arm in the air and basically yelling, "Penny's here," across hall.

Fighting the urge to throw his hand over Silvia's mouth, to shut her up, Seth watched Mr. and Mrs. Roberts head in their direction.

Before her parents reached them, Silvia gushed, "I'm so excited, in one week, I get to walk down the aisle with Braden."

In a teasing tone that was lost on Silvia, Penny replied, "Well that's what I'm most looking forward to at the wedding."

"I know right! Braden is so hot."

Smiling at the way Penny scrunched up her face at Silvia's response, Seth noticed the Roberts' had joined them.

Mrs. Roberts closed her eyes and shook her head at Silvia having overheard her comment about Braden at the same time Mr. Roberts extended his hand to Seth.

"It's good to see you again Seth."

"Thank you sir."

Penny's tone was soft as she stood up tall greeting, "Mr. and Mrs. Roberts."

"You better give me a hug," Mrs. Roberts fussed at Penny.

With a slight giggle, Penny hugged her saying, "Hi Amila."

Mr. Roberts leaned closer to Seth warning, "I would keep my arm around her if I were you. Otherwise someone might steal her away."

Seth noticed Penny blush as she replied, "Emerson."
With his nerves already on edge, Seth felt his pulse quicken at the mere thought of that happening.

A stinging sensation radiated down the side of his arm as Mr. Roberts gave it a good smack, assuring, "Relax, I was only joking."
Seth forced a smile, but it quickly faded as Ellis Montgomery joined them.

Chairman of The Society and the granddaughter of The Society's founder meant Ellis Montgomery came from money. Old money. She was graceful, elegant but tolerated little. Her position allowed her the privilege of making or breaking anyone who was interested in climbing the ladder of high society.

Immediately greeting Mrs. Roberts first, she gave her a short embrace.

"Amila dear, you are absolutely lovely this evening."

"Ellis," Mrs. Roberts replied back with a genuine smile and a friendly tone.

She then greeted Mr. Roberts, "Emerson, you are looking as handsome as ever."

Giving her a nod he replied, "Always a pleasure to see you."

Waving him off as if his compliment was unnecessary, Mrs. Montgomery informed, "I am afraid the two of you are needed at the auction table."
Departing smiles were given as the Roberts' stepped away.

Mrs. Montgomery turned to Seth and Penny almost smirking as she extended her hand toward Penny.

"Ellis Montgomery."

Lightly shaking it, Penny replied, "Penny Caffrey."

Nodding as if she already knew who his date was and was just going through the proper formalities, Mrs. Montgomery released her hand stating, "I adored your father."

Penny's face beamed at the compliment.

"And Seth, have you spoken to your parents yet?"

"No ma'am."

"Well, it appears as though your luck has run out."

Seth gave her a confused expression before hearing, "Mrs. Montgomery."

Glancing to the side, he noticed the fake smiles plastered across his mother and father's faces as they approached.

Feeling Penny's hand make its way around to the inside of his elbow, a knot formed in the pit of Seth's stomach.

"Linda," Mrs. Montgomery replied, sounding put out by his mother's presence.

Sneering down at Penny, Linda greeted, "And you are?"

"Penny Caffrey," she replied with a smile on her face while tightening her hold on his arm.

Looking unimpressed, Linda turned to Seth's father reminding him, "The one that works at the tattoo parlor."

Mrs. Montgomery quickly broke in questioning, "Do you now?"

"Yes ma'am. I am apprenticing at my cousin's shop, Legacy Ink."

Leonard turned his head away in disgust admonishing, "A deplorable and filthy profession that causes infection and spreads disease."

Before Seth could think of a way to get them away from this insulting situation, Penny stated, "That's not true."

Appearing angry, Leonard barked, "I beg your pardon."

There was a light smile to her expression as Penny explained, "Our needles come prepackaged and sterilized. They are disposed of after each use to prevent the spread of disease just like in hospitals and doctor's offices." Leonard's face grew red at the comparison as Penny continued, "And since the needle of a tattoo gun only breaks the third layer of skin, which is around one sixteenth of a paper plate deep, you actually have a better chance of getting an infection from a paper cut than you do a tattoo."

Seth's father appeared livid as his mother stood there in shock.

A tall man made his way up to Mrs. Montgomery, placing his hand against her back as he leaned close to her, privately speaking to in her ear.

She gave him a nod as he stepped away before sharing, "If you will excuse me."

Penny cheered, "It was nice to meet you," before Mrs. Montgomery replied, "It was an absolute pleasure, dear."

The knot that had formed in Seth's stomach twisted as Mrs. Montgomery stepped away leaving him and Penny with his parents.

Even though Seth was a few inches taller than his father, he felt like he was shrinking under his domineering stare. Beads of sweat formed at his temples while his collar started to strangle him.

"You have invested nothing in this family and now you're intent on publically embarrassing me?"

Leonard's words came in less of a question and more as a statement of fact.

A suffocating feeling started to overtake Seth as he choked out, "No sir..." before Penny replied, "I wasn't trying to be rude."

The polite smile returned to her face as she rambled, "There are many common misconceptions about tattoos. For instance, did you know..."

"Why are you still speaking," Linda coldly stated with a smile to keep up appearances.

Seth looked down at Penny seeing her face flush with embarrassment as her hand loosen from around his arm before falling to her side.

He could tell Penny was working hard at keeping her composure as she tilted her head down, glancing off to the side, when Leonard demanded, "Keep your distance this evening."

"Yes sir."

The air around them lifted slightly the moment his parents stepped away. That was until he turned to Penny and saw the expression on her face.

Seth watched her chest rise and fall in a rapid rhythm as she kept her head down. He felt low, dirty even. He had let his parents talk down to his sweet beautiful Penny. Like the coward that he was, he allowed them to make her feel lesser than them with no defense. When the truth was, he was the lesser of the four and his lame, 'Yes sir' was all he needed to prove it.

As the night went on, Penny appeared to recover while Seth did not. In the car on the way back to his apartment, he tugged at the knot of his bowtie. When he finally broke it free from around his neck, he unbuttoned the first two buttons of his shirt, hoping to breathe easier.

Penny had been very quiet until they entered his apartment. Following him to the kitchen she remained next to his table while he continued to get himself a bottle of water from the refrigerator.

"Maybe if I invited your parents over for dinner..."

Spinning around in shock Seth griped, "Are you out of your mind?"

Her expression bordered on being insulted as she answered, "I knew going into it that tattoos aren't something everyone is comfortable with. It's something some people look down on and worse for me because I'm a woman, especially around here. That's why most of my family doesn't know."

"You think that's what this is about?"

With a thoughtful smile, she replied, "You saw how my mom reacted when she found out I had one. She doesn't know I work there. Auggie doesn't even know I'm apprenticing, he thinks I'm just there to sweep the floors or whatever."

Infuriated with her optimism, Seth fussed, "They will never like you."

"But if they got to know me..."

"You think that matters?"

Sounding wounded, Penny replied, "I just thought..."

"No. You walk around in this little fantasy world acting like at the end of the day everything will be alright no matter what. That's not real life Penny. Look at my family. My own father disinherited me because I didn't want to be him. I don't want to subject you to how you're going to be treated by my father and mother just by being with me. How could you want that? Look at your family. You know how your mom treats Charlotte and Liv. You want that? Because you're a fool if you do."

He could see the tears building in her eyes as she shared, "I just think that if two people love each other none of that is supposed to matter. I mean, I would make a fool outta myself in front of the entire world if that's what it took to be with you."

Fed up with the conversation, her overly positive outlook, his parents and himself, Seth stated, "Well I'm not you," before turning his back to her.

⌘

Standing next to Seth's kitchen table, Penny stared at his back. She waited a moment for him to turn around. When he didn't, she frowned feeling the dreaded inevitable.

There were things she wanted to say to him and questions she felt she had the right to ask, but as the realization that this was the end sunk in, she didn't see the point.

Agreeing to the breakup Penny said, "Okay," and walked out of his apartment.
Meaning to move faster, she slowly walked across the balcony to her door.

Sitting on the edge of her bed, Penny pulled the bobby pins out of her hair, allowing it to fall down around her shoulders. Sweeping the length over one shoulder, she looked at the double heart marked on her wrist. Holding the bottom of her hair in her hand, she brushed her finger across the ends. Remembering the things he said that made her fall before they were replaced with the words that made her hit the ground, Penny started to cry.

Twenty Eight

Reaching his arm out, Seth expected to feel warmth and softness next to him, instead of the emptiness he found. He was dreaming about Penny. Her back against his chest, his face buried in her hair with nothing between them as he slid his arms around her waist to pull her closer before his mind slowly reminded him why he was empty handed. Squeezing his eyes closed, he started to hyperventilate.

The last three mornings had gone exactly the same. Sweet dreams of her followed by a harsh reality resulting in the worst anxiety attacks he had ever experienced.

Sunday morning, he had knocked on her door without receiving an answer and five more times throughout the day with the same result. Monday afternoon, he walked into Legacy Ink but was immediately, not so politely, asked to leave by Liv. Tuesday evening, he ran into Charlotte on the balcony and was told to keep his distance in a rather threatening manner. Today, he was going to try again. She would leave her apartment to go to work any minute now, and he was going to be right there waiting when she did.

Waiting, Seth spent the next hour glancing between his phone and her door. When her door finally opened, Seth's entire body seized up. It wasn't Penny who stepped out onto the balcony. Shorter than Seth but close to six foot tall he had brown shaggy hair and was wearing a black t-shirt and cargo pants with flip flops. Feeling his breathing pick up Seth watched him lean back into the open doorway.

Suddenly irrational, Seth hoped that he was there for Charlotte and not Penny. There was some guilt in the thinking that his own heartache could be soothed by another man being wounded but it quickly became an afterthought the second he heard Penny's voice.

A sweet sounding, "Bye," from her made his stomach turn and mentally made him an invisible part of their conversation.

"See you Friday."

What's happening Friday?

"Sorry I kept you up so late."

Late? How late?

Bile rose in Seth's throat as Penny replied, "It was worth it. You are amazing."

No, he's not.

"I'm really not."

See!

"The things you do are."

Unable to stomach anymore, Seth pulled his keys out of his pocket, locked his door, swiftly walked past Penny and Cargo Pants Guy before heading down the stairs to the parking lot.

He needed to take his mind off of everything and spending the day he took off, in hopes of making up with Penny, alone in his apartment would not have done him any good. The only place he had to go was work. There he could get lost in never-ending numbers and pretend he hadn't lost her.

Sitting behind his desk, he had received a few strange looks for wearing a button down and khaki's instead of a suit. It was business as usual, until the intercom on his phone buzzed.

"Yes sir?"

"Come in my office."

"Yes sir."

Pushing away from his desk, Seth stood up and walked into Jackson's office.

Motioning for Seth to sit the moment he walked him, Jackson had a frustrated expression on his face.

"Didn't I give you the day off?"

Taking a seat facing the desk, Seth replied, "Yes sir."

Raising his eyebrows as he folded his hands on top of his desk, Jackson questioned, "Then why are you here?"

After wondering how he could be in trouble for not taking the day off, Seth replied, "My plans fell through."
Jackson leaned back in his chair before smiling wide as he shook his head at Seth.

"Do you want to talk about it?"

Feeling very uncomfortable Seth answered, "Not particularly."

Nodding Jackson shared, "Well, unfortunately for you, Ren thinks you should."

Thinking this had to be in some way unethical, Seth replied, "Mr. Thomas, I..."

Holding his hand up, Jackson explained, "I already know the story so we can start with why you broke up with Penny?"

"I'm not entirely sure I did. I wasn't trying to, but I think she took it that way."

"So, you had a bad night, freaked out a little and started talking out of your ass. She of course took it like your hand was on the Bible, and now she won't give you the chance to make it right."
Seth stared at him in awe. That was exactly what happened.

"Mind if I give you some advice?"

"No sir."

"Nothing beats a sincere apology and depending on the woman, flowers are a nice touch."

Nodding at Jackson, Seth wondered if he should bring up the guy leaving Penny's this morning and get some advice on that also.

As Seth sat there debating on whether or not to share Penny's alleged promiscuous activities, the phone on Jackson's desk buzzed.

"Trent Roberts is here to see you."

Pressing a button on his phone, Jackson replied, "Send him back."

Seth knew his time with Jackson was up for now, so he decided against adding to the conversation.

As soon as his door opened, Jackson stood up and greeted, "Dang boy, I swear you get taller every time I see you."

Seth immediately stood, unable to believe who had just walked in.

"Jacks," Trent greeted shaking his hand before giving him a one-sided hug.

Narrowing his eyes at them, Seth mentally growled, Cargo Pants Guy.

Watching his boss smile at Mr. Supposedly Amazing, Seth started to feel territorial. First Penny now Jackson. Who was this guy?

In answer to his mental question, Jackson introduced, "Trent, this is Seth, he's my right-hand man," then patting Trent on the back he said, "And this kid here, he's amazing."

Too engrossed in the memory of him standing outside Penny's door to respond he gave a nod and continued staring at them.

Jackson gave Seth a curious scowl before turning back to Trent asking, "So how does it feel to be back home?"

With a shrug and a laugh, Trent replied, "I'll let you know when I make it there. My flight was so late getting in, I didn't want to wake mom and dad so I crashed at Charlotte's."

"Are you headed there now?"

"I'm going to swing by the foundation to see dad and drop my slides off before I do," Trent answered before sharing, "Penny stayed up until four in the morning helping me put them back in order."

Seth let out a sigh of relief.

He hadn't made the connection at first. Trent was Charlotte's younger brother, and now that Seth was sure he hadn't slept with Penny, he could admit the guy was pretty amazing. He devoted all his free time to underprivileged children, working with outreach programs and help centers across the country.

Breaking into their conversation, Seth walked over and held his hand out to Trent.

"It is good to meet you," he stated shaking his hand before turning to Jackson and asking, "Can I still take the day?"

Smiling wide, Jackson replied, "You sure can."

Seth was still at square one, but it wasn't over until he had the chance to talk to Penny. Leaving JPT Financial, he headed straight for the flower shop.

Staring out of his peephole, with a bouquet of wild roses in his hand, Seth waited. It had only been around thirty minutes but if felt like hours when he saw the top of Penny's head over the railing. Because of the position of his door, it was hard to see her after a certain point so he waited a minute before stepping out onto the balcony.

Quickly walking up to her, Penny glanced in his direction but didn't make eye contact. It was obvious she was trying to hurry and get inside.

"Penny."

In her haste, she dropped her keys. Seth reached for them, but she quickly snatched them up and shoved her key into the door.

"Talk to me," be urged trying to stop her before she made it inside.

Turning her doorknob Penny shook her head.

Holding the flowers he bought between her and the door he apologized, "I'm sorry. I didn't mean what I said."

Cracking her door open she stopped, turning her head in his direction without looking at him.

"You sat on your bed and promised me that you didn't say things you didn't mean."

"I know I did. Penny please, I didn't ..."

"Then you're a liar?"

Admittedly she had him backed into a corner.

"No, I guess in a way I did mean it but I..."

Seth paused trying to think of the right words to say when she ended it.

"I don't want to be friends with you anymore."

Stepping into her apartment, she closed the door on him.

Seth stared at her door for a few moments before setting the flowers he bought her on the balcony in front of her door. Slowly walking back to his apartment, he was devastated. He hadn't just lost a friend or even a girlfriend, losing Penny meant losing the rest of his life with her in it.

Twenty Nine

Sitting on the couch in Ren and Jackson's living room, Penny held Keylee on her lap. It had been several months since she had seen her niece, her childhood friend, Sophia or her brother Ailin. Penny was glad they were down for the wedding, she welcomed the distraction from Seth.

Since meeting Charlotte, Penny had grown closer to her than she ever was growing up with Sophia. Mainly due to the fact that her friendship with Sophia, for the most part was one sided. Sophia was a little on the snotty side but spending time with her would be a nice change of pace since both Charlotte and Liv wouldn't let what happened with Seth go.

Liv was the first to make her feelings known when she shared that she didn't like making him leave the shop and that Penny needed to talk to him. She was a hypocrite sometimes. The very next day Charlotte followed suit telling her, she was on her side and enjoyed threatening him as punishment for being stupid. She also felt Seth at least deserved the right to explain himself.

Penny understood where they were coming from and if it wasn't her, she more than likely would have given the same advice. But the fact was, it was herself she was concerned about and yesterday when he caught her going into her apartment, and tried to double talk his way back with her, was all the proof she needed. Seth may have gone about it differently than the others, in the scheme of things, he was just another failed relationship.

Penny swiped a few strands away from Keylee's face as she slept, nestled against her arm.

"She's getting so big."

With a nod, Sophia informed, "Next month she will be a year old."

"And she still looks just like Ailin...Poor baby," Penny laughed.

Laughing with her, Sophia replied, "I know, if she didn't have brown hair, I would think my genes are clear or something."

"It could be worse, she could look just like Auggie," Penny teased, noticing her brother walk by.

"Hey," Auggie griped, causing Keylee to jerk away and look up at him.

"You woke her up," Sophia fussed at him as her niece sniffled before starting to cry.

Pulling her closer, Penny patted her saying, "It's okay, I won't let that scary man get you."

As Auggie gave his sister a dirty look, Keylee squirmed in Penny's lap holding her arms out to him.

"Scary my ass, I'm her favorite uncle," he assured before Sophia fussed, "Don't curse in front of her, Auggie," as she rolled her eyes and shook her head.

Scooping his niece up in his arms, Auggie smiled at her saying, "Come on girly, let's go see Aunt Charlotte," as he walked away with her.

Penny looked at Sophia with fake sincerity stating, "I am very concerned with your parenting skills if Auggie is her favorite."

"It's the beard," Sophia shared with a laugh.

Laughing with her, Penny thought this was nice and exactly what she needed.

They sat silent for a few minutes causing Penny's mind to drift back to Seth.

As if Sophia knew why Penny had started to scowl, she asked, "Is Seth still coming with you Saturday?"

"No."

A curious smile formed as she questioned, "What happened to staying friends with exes?"

Shaking her head, Penny's heart started to hurt. That had actually gone out the window when she found out Brooks was cheating on her with Lily.

"It's for the best you know, I always thought that was kinda strange, staying friends with an ex and all."

Shrugging, Penny replied, "Yea..."

Penny's mood had noticeably changed this time causing an uncomfortable silence between them.

Not long after Charlotte and Auggie left to open the bar, Sarah arrived. No one mentioned Charlotte, Auggie or the wedding until dinner was over. Then to everyone's surprise, it was Sarah, who had been against it since before Auggie even proposed, who brought it up.

The dining room went silent as Penny's mom looked at her and shared, "I can't wait to see Seth Saturday. He can sit with me during the service."

Since she had purposely left Sarah out of the break up loop, all eyes fell on Penny.

"Umm, he won't be there."

"Why not?" Sarah questioned with a glare.

Looking down at the table, she replied, "We're not together anymore."

"Why not?" Sarah repeated.

Feeling put on the spot, Penny knew everyone else knew but she didn't want to talk about it in front of everyone or at all for that matter.

"We broke up."

"Seriously Penny, he's the first respectable man you've ever been with and..." Sarah fussed before Penny snapped back saying, "He broke up with me."

"Why would he do that?" she questioned appearing shocked.

Feeling as if she was about to cry, Penny answered, "His parents don't like me."

Offended, Sarah griped, "Why not? What's wrong with you?"

Penny knew her mom meant her question as to be on her side, but the fact that she had been asking herself that question since they broke up, made it hurt.

"I don't know," she replied barely above a whisper before pushing away from the table and leaving the room.

Standing on the back patio, Penny stared out into the yard. Why was this so hard? It had been a few days and she should have been well on her way to recovery by now. After Brooks she had decided to stop dating for a while and she still felt that way but this was different. She had made a choice to focus more on herself than being in a relationship after Brooks and to be honest, she wasn't that upset that they broke up. Sure she was disappointed over the break up and then angry when she found out she had been cheated on but this thing with Seth, it being over was different. It had ended, that wasn't breaking news, her relationships always did. This one though, left her feeling empty and that was a first.

The worst part was, she didn't want to go home. Knowing he was next door just made it worse. Not to mention, she had practically turned into a hermit trying to avoid him. It wasn't fair. She lived there first. The first place she'd lived all on her own. Well, maybe not all on her own since she was roommates with Charlotte and now Braden was there, but still. How dare him.

Just as she felt herself getting good and mad over the outcome of her and Seth's whatever it was, Penny heard the patio door open.

"Hey Pen-Pen, you okay?"

Rolling her eyes, she griped, "I'm great."

Walking around to face her, Braden laughed, "I figured you were. You don't look upset at all."

Looking at him like he was stupid, she replied, "Shut up."

Continuing to smile he offered, "Know what would make you feel better? Getting hammered at The Dog House."

"You know I don't drink, stupid," finding it a little hard to keep a straight face.

"Then being designated driver for your favorite brother will definitely do the trick," Braden assured with a silly grin across his face.

Without being able to help it, she smiled, "Really?"

Wrapping an arm around her shoulders, he added, "Be nice if I wasn't the odd man out for a change."

Scowling at him, Penny teased, "You know, asking your sister out on a date is strange even for you."

Letting go of her, Braden threw his hands in the air saying, "Hey, desperate times call for desperate measures."

"That's sick Braden!" Penny practically shouted while bursting into laughter.

Nodding in agreement and smiling with pride for cheering her up, he put his arm back around her leading her back inside.

The Dog House was packed when Penny and Braden arrived. Luckily, Kieran and Liv were already at the bar and they were able to squeeze in next to them. Charlotte stayed out of the manager's office most of the night and hung out behind the bar next to Auggie. It was fun and Penny started to feel like her normal self for the first time since things ended with Seth.

After closing, Braden, Kieran and Liv hung out in the main area of the bar while Auggie closed up. Penny headed to the back to hang out with Charlotte.

Watching Charlotte balance out the night's receipts, Penny sat in the chair facing the desk.

"In thirty-four hours you'll be a Caffrey, You ready?"

"Yes!" she blurted before adding, "But I will miss living with you."

Smiling at her, Penny replied, "It won't be that different. We're always together anyway."

"True, but your food tastes so much better than his."

Laughing, Penny shared, "I've been cooking a whole lot longer than he has and I still have no idea how you got him to start anyway."

"Oh that was easy. I just explained to him that the only thing I know how to make is scrambled eggs so unless he wanted to eat them for the rest of his life, he should learn how to cook."

With a suspicious expression, she questioned, "And that really worked?"

A secretive smile answered more than Penny cared to know as Charlotte replied, "Other promises concerning dessert may have been made."

Penny wrinkled her nose and made a disgusted face as Charlotte started to laugh. They both sat still for a moment when they heard shouting coming from the main area of the bar.

Running through the swinging doors at the same time, Penny rushed right up to the fight as Charlotte made her way over at a slower pace.

Auggie was holding on to Braden from behind with arms across his chest, growling, "I said knock it off."

Liv was facing Kieran with her hand on his chest shouting, "Stop it!" at him.

Before Penny could ask what was happening, Braden griped, "You're a sorry ass mother f..." when Liv cut him off agreeing, "Yea that's a dirty thing to do."

"Why ya takin' his side?" Kieran barked at Liv.

"You're wrong for making her think..." Liv fussed before stopping when Auggie alerted, "Liv."

"What am I missing?" Penny asked as the four of them looked at her like they'd been caught.

Jerking away from his brother, Braden took a step closer to Penny saying, "Nothin' Pen, let's go."

Shaking her head at him, she looked at all of them asking, "This is about me?"

Everyone stared at her before Braden nodded saying, "Guess no one else is man enough, I'll tell you."

"Braden," Auggie snapped before Braden turned around and hollered, "You should be just as mad as I am."

Auggie instantly yelled back, "I'm not gonna tell the man what he can and can't do in his shop."

"Did Penny say that to you when mom refused to draw out your tattoo or did..."

Cringing Penny heard Charlotte shout, "What?"
Auggie instantly grabbed the front of his brother's shirt.

Auggie looked like he was about to murder Braden when Charlotte shoved him away and stood in front of Auggie.

"She refused?" Charlotte questioned with an angry glare.

"Lotte..."Auggie started before Charlotte narrowed her eye at him fussing, "I cannot believe you."

Scowling Auggie looked like he had no idea what to say then, pointed at Braden swearing, "Your dumbass is out of the wedding."

Braden appeared genuinely wounded before Charlotte looked at him assuring, "No you're not," then back at Auggie saying, "No he's not."

"The hell he's not," Auggie griped.

Narrowing her eyes at him, Charlotte questioned, "Do you wanna marry me?"

With a stunned expression on his face, Auggie nodded.

"Then he's in the wedding," Charlotte informed before turning and heading out of the room.

Quickly behind her, he asked, "Where are you going?"

"To see your mother," Charlotte snapped causing Auggie to stop dead in his tracks.

Turning back to them he looked at his brother and warned, "I better not see your ass before three on Saturday," before taking off after Charlotte.

It was silent in the bar before Penny put all the pieces of their argument together.

Looking at Braden, she asked, "Does Auggie know I'm apprenticing?" as he nodded she asked, "How?"

Shooting a dirty look at Kieran, he spouted, "Ask the vault over there."

"Boy you better..." Kieran snapped before Liv fussed, "Be honest for once in your life."

Swallowing hard, Penny said, "I asked you not to tell him."

Kieran's jaw flexed as he looked away from her.

Braden shook his head saying, "I'll be in the car," before passing Liv mumbling, "And you call me a punk."

Once again the bar was silent.

Glancing between Liv and Kieran, Penny frowned.

"Did you know Kieran told him?"

"Yea, I did," Liv answered.

Focusing back on Kieran, Penny asked, "Why did you tell him?"

"You're his little sister, I wouldn't have felt right about hiding it from him."

"So it's just Auggie your honest with and everyone else can go to hell is that right?"

Appearing agitated at Penny's tone, Kieran replied, "I have a responsibility in preserving my trade. It's not just something I woke up one day and thought it would be cool to do. It's my legacy."

"Oh shut up!" Penny snapped before griping, "You can spout that legacy crap all you want but you only up hold it when it's convenient for you!"

"That's right and while I'm being honest, I told your brother 'cause I figured he'd say no!"
Penny was so stunned by what he said, she physically took a step back.

"You don't want me in your shop?" she questioned in a shaky voice as a tear rolled down her cheek.

"Penny, I love having you at the shop," he said apologetically before admitting, "You don't have any business tattooing there."
Shaking her head at him, Penny tried blinking the tears back but it was no use.

Glancing at Liv, who looked horrified at what her husband had just shared, Penny continued shaking her head as she turned to leave the bar.

She heard Liv blurt, "You're an asshole," as she rushed to her side.

"What do ya want me to do Liv," Kieran griped from behind them before Liv whipped her head around demanding, "Fix it!" before walking with Penny out of the bar.

When Penny and Liv made it to Braden's El Camino, he was passed out in the passenger seat. Making her way to the driver's side, Penny leaned her back against the door and frowned.

"He was right," Penny sniffled as Liv wiped her hair away from her tear stained face.

"Who was right beautiful?"

213

"I am a fool...Nothing ever turns out and I..."

Placing her hands on the sides of Penny's face, Liv looked her directly in the eyes saying, "You listen to me. You're the only one of us that's not a fool. You make your own sunshine. None of us know how to do that. You find happiness when there isn't any. That's not foolish, it's a miracle. You make all of our lives better just by being you."

"Maybe I should start drinking," Penny replied, still hurt but feeling a little better.

Pulling her into a hug, Liv laughed, "Nah, if you start drinkin' they'll be no one to drive Braden's dumbass home." Smiling, she hugged Liv back.

Pulling away from The Dog House, Penny reached to turn the radio on when Braden swatted her hand away.

"I thought you were asleep."

"Just thinkin' with my eyes closed."

"If you say so."

"Liv's right ya know."

Nodding, Penny replied, "I know...You really are a dumbass."

Thirty

Lying in her bed, Penny held her own wrist in her hand staring at her tattoo. Pressing her thumb against it, she could feel her pulse. Closing her eyes, she remembered Seth saying 'I can feel your heart beat' right before he kissed her for the first time. The longer she thought about him, the sadder she became but this time, she wasn't sad for herself. She still had her family and he had no one. After dwelling on that for a moment, she hopped out of bed, ready to start a brand new day.

Braden was curled up on the couch sleeping as Penny headed towards her front door. Stopping a moment to watch him sleep, her heart was sad for him too. He was lost. Caught between what he always wanted and what he never really had, her brother was hanging in the balance. He needed someone, a friend.

Making her way to the couch, she crouched down and tapped him on the forehead.

"Braden."

Stretching his arm over the side of his face, he groaned, "I'm asleep."

"Braden."

He breathed out a loud sigh before griping, "What?"

"You never said anything about Seth breaking up with me."

Sliding his arm down he kept his eyes closed as he scowled at her saying, "There's nothing to say."

"So you're indifferent?"

"I'm your brother."

Nodding, she asked, "Can you do me a favor?"

"Will you let me go back to sleep if I say yes?"

Rolling her eyes, she said, "Sure."

There was a pause before he griped, "What is it?"

Taking a deep breath before blowing it out, Penny asked, "Can you check on Seth?"

"You want me to go check on him?"

"Yea," she snapped before explaining, "He doesn't have anyone."

"Whose fault is that?"

There was a slight sting in his words causing Penny to question, "What's that supposed to mean?"

Shaking his head, Braden rolled over answering, "Nothin' Pen, I'll check on him for you."

Hopping up, she assured, "It's not for me."

"Whatever you say."

Placing her hand on her hip, she sneered down at him, insisting, "It's not!"

"Okay, it's not. I believe you. Now let me go back to sleep."

Letting out a loud frustrated groan, Penny stomped over to her door and walked out, slamming it behind herself.

The bell above the door at Legacy Ink rang as Penny walked in.

"'Morning," she cheered seeing Liv smile at her before stepping to the back.

Walking behind the counter, she noticed Kieran at his station. When he didn't look up at her, she tossed her purse under the counter and checked the calendar for appointments.

Thinking Kieran must be working on art for the morning's first appointment, it was unusual for someone to schedule that early, but it looked like Liv had been the one to mark it down. Moving to his station to start setups, she stopped when he turned around in his chair.

"What are you doing?"

Trying not to make a face at him, she said, "Your set-ups... you have an appointment in thirty minutes."

"I'm doin' 'em myself today," he replied before turning back to his table.

Sticking her tongue out at the back of his head, she mentally blurted 'Jerk!' before heading back behind the counter.

Thirty minutes came and went while Penny stood behind the counter.

With a heavy sigh, she asked, "Do you want me to scratch Mr. Ass... Assat... Um, that can't be right... I don't know how to pronounce it. Anyways, it doesn't look like the guy's gonna show up."

Giving her a confused glare, Kieran stood up and walked to the counter.

"What does it say?"

Shrugging Penny replied, "It's Liv's handwriting."

He leaned over and looked at the calendar before hollering to the back, "Liv!"

Stepping in from the back, she asked, "What's up?"

"Mr. Ass-hat?"

Glancing up like she was trying to think, she replied, "Ya know, it's possible he goes by a different name but when he was talking that's what kept popping into my mind."

Covering his face with his hand, Kieran shook his head and started to laugh.

Seeing Liv's smirk as Kieran continued to laugh, Penny raised her eyebrows and looked off to the side thinking, 'Yea, that's not weird at all'.

Still shaking his head at Liv, Kieran walked back to his station saying, "Mr. Ass-hat isn't my client. He's yours," to Penny as he sat down in the in the opposite chair.

Caught off guard, Penny asked, "What?"

Pushing his stool towards her with his foot, Kieran replied, "You want it or not."

Speechless, Penny frantically nodded at him.

⌘

Flipping through channels, Seth stopped on Yesterday to Today: Ancient Civilization's Impact on the Modern World. Leaning his head back against the couch, he closed his eyes and listened to the documentary. It didn't take long for him to recall the last time it was on. That was the first night he made it into Penny's top ten.

Two minutes in, he couldn't stand it anymore and turned the TV off. Seth was miserable. No, beyond miserable. Unsure what was worse than miserable, whatever it was, that's what he was.

Tossing his remote on the couch, he stood up and walked into his kitchen. Pulling out a box of coco puffs, he turned and opened his cabinet. Staring right at him was Penny's black and white polka dot bowl. With a heavy sigh, he closed the cabinet. Walking back to his living room, Seth stuck his hand down into the cereal box and retrieved a hand full of the chocolate puffs just as there was a knock at his door.

He had no intentions of answering the door but decided to check and see who it was anyway. Shoving a hand full of cereal into his mouth, Seth looked out of the peephole. Chewing, he stepped back and stared at his door. Another knock and he paused before looking out of the peephole again. Tucking the box of cereal to his chest with one hand, he turned the doorknob with the other.

"What's goin' on, man?" Braden asked as soon as Seth opened his door.

Shrugging, Seth grabbed another hand full of cereal, "Do you want to come in?" before eating it.

"Yea...You okay there?" Braden asked as he stepped inside.

Nodding, Seth offered him some coco puffs as he held the box out to him.

With a slight laugh, Braden said, "Nah, man, I'm good." Thinking suit yourself, he sat back down on the couch.

Another hand full of cereal mixed with a concerned look from Braden caused Seth's stomach to hurt.

Taking a seat on the other end of the couch, Braden shared, "Looks like you've got a fun night of eating coco puffs alone in the dark ahead of you, so I'll make this quick."

Leaning his head back against the couch, Seth asked, "Is it about Penny?"

"Sorta."

Seth looked over at him saying, "I don't mean to be unfriendly Braden but I'd rather be alone."

"Than with Penny?"

"No," he quickly replied before informing, "She's the one that ended things."

"I know she did and I can't help you."

Seth couldn't help giving him a stupid look as he snapped, "Well, thanks for stopping by."

"Anytime," Braden laughed.

It wasn't that Seth didn't like Braden, he got along with him fine but at the moment he didn't find him amusing.

"Shouldn't you be at the rehearsal dinner?"

"Should be. I got myself uninvited," he replied with a 'Whatever' expression before saying, "It's cool though, I've got a date instead."

Looking at Braden, he started to wonder why he'd come over in the first place.

Braden slapped his hands against his knees before standing up.

Standing up too, Seth shared, "I'm sorry, I..."

"I know man, I can't imagine not havin' Penny in my life and I'm just her brother."

Now he was just being cruel, Seth thought, cringing at his statement.

"It funny ya know..." Braden said trailing off as he walked to the door.

"What is?"

With his hand on the knob, he continued, "How two people can want the exact same thing but neither is willing to take the risk."

"I tried..." Seth replied unsure if he was trying to convince Braden or himself.

Nodding he suggested, "Well man, if you tried, you tried. That's all you can do. Right?"

Seth didn't have it in him to agree as he watched Braden open his door to leave.

"Besides, I'm not the brother you should be talkin' to anyway," he shared before stepping out and closing the door behind himself.

⌘

Liv was sitting on a bench off to the side while the wedding party prepared for the wedding rehearsal when Penny arrived. In a fantastic mood after Kieran's approval of her artwork on his arm, and then Charlotte's wedding present being ready to pick up, she skipped up to Liv.

"What are you doing way over here?"

Hopping up, Liv replied, "Waitin' for you, Beautiful."

Penny gave her a suspicious scowl.

"Fine, I'm tryin' to keep my mouth shut."

With a laugh, she blurted, "Since when?"

"About ten minutes ago," Liv laughed in response before saying, "Come on you'll see."

Confused, Penny walked with Liv over to where everyone else was standing.

The closer they made it to everyone, the more obvious it was that Liv wasn't the only one keeping their distance from the wedding party.

As soon as they walked up, Charlotte stated, "Penny's here, let's get this over with."

Everyone instantly obeyed, moving to their positions.

Charlotte's youngest sister Lola made her way down the aisle first carrying an empty flower basket. Penny walked arm in arm with Kieran meeting Auggie where the altar would be in the morning. Silvia pouted as she made her way next to Penny all by herself. Next came Charlotte's other sister Jenna with Ailin. Lastly, Emerson walked his seemingly disgruntled daughter down the aisle.

With everyone in place, Reverend Gary, who also happened to be a Caffrey, started the rehearsal ceremony.

Just as he was getting to dearly beloved, Auggie looked over at Kieran asking, "Is that a yellow heart?"

"Yep," Kieran replied before Penny cheered, "Did you check out the smiley face in it?" referring to the fresh tattoo she had giving him at the top of his forearm.

Shaking his head with a laugh, Auggie said, "I should have known."

Penny's proud smile at the moment was cut short when Reverend Gary cleared his throat saying, "If you don't mind."

Ignoring him, Charlotte leaned closer to Kieran to inspect the tattoo before complimenting, "Wow, that looks great Penny."

Reverend Gary glared at Charlotte's continued interruption as Auggie griped, "You can stop lookin' at her like that."

"Don't defend me," she snapped before apologizing, "I'm sorry Reverend, please continue."

Auggie growled under his breath before a scowl took over his expression. Penny drew in a deep breath thinking 'This can't be good'.

The 'I do's' consisted of a 'Yea' from Auggie and a 'Whatever' from Charlotte. When that was over Charlotte and Auggie turned to head back down the aisle. Penny noticed him reach to take her hand and watched her refuse it with a loud huff before taking off without him.

Blowing out an exasperated breath over her almost sister in law and brother, Penny headed towards the couple.

Seeing the discontent on their faces, she decided to intervene.

"So is everyone as excited as I am for tomorrow?" she cheered.

They both stared at her with unpleasant expressions.

"There is going to be a wedding tomorrow, right?"

Charlotte gave the bottom of her shirt a little tug before saying, "Well I don't know. Augustus could get mad at me and tell me not to show up," before walking off.

"Damn it Charlotte," he griped, taking off after her.

With a heavy sigh, Penny shook her head at them.

⌘

It was a little after one in the morning before Seth was able to work up the nerve to have a conversation with the brother Braden advised he should talk to. After driving by Auggie's house and seeing the driveway empty, he tried the next logical place he thought he would find him.

When Seth walked into The Dog House, he saw Auggie sitting at a table in the corner with a bottle of whiskey and a glass in front of him.

"Bar's closed," he informed without looking up from his glass.

Taking a few controlled breaths, Seth walked towards him.

"I want to be with Penny," he forced out feeling anxious.

Lifting his glass, Auggie replied, "Good for you," before taking a sip.

Unsure of himself, he asked, "What do I do?"

Setting his glass down, Auggie answered, "Prove it."

Confused, Seth questioned, "How do I do that?"

"Be a man," Auggie griped before getting up from his chair and glaring at him.

This was one of the last things Seth ever wanted to do but if he needed to earn Auggie's respect to get Penny back then that's what he was going to do.

Rolling up his sleeves, Seth tried to prepare himself for the beating he was sure to get.

With a deep controlled inhale, he said, "I'm ready."

Auggie scowled before shaking his head at him.

"Boy sit your ass down, I'm not fixin' to fight you," he fussed as he made his way behind the bar.

Relieved beyond any measure, Seth quickly took a seat at the table.

Still shaking his head, as he made his way back to the table, Auggie set a glass in front of Seth, and poured him a drink.

Sitting back down in his chair, Auggie filled his own glass before saying, "Let's hear it."

A million things raced through Seth's mind, but all he could say was, "She's the one."

Nodding, Auggie sipped his whiskey before offering, "Shouldn't you be tellin' her that?"

"She won't listen."

Auggie nodded again before covering his mouth with his hand and running it down the front of his bread sharing, "We're an interesting bunch ya know. Braden's always got his head up his ass, Ailin's had his up Sophia's since he was a teenager and me, I'm just a plain ol' ass in general."

Seth continued to listen as Auggie seemed to talk more to himself than to him.

"Even Will, God rest him, had his moments... Then there's Penny. How the hell she ended up in our bunch, I'll never know."

"There's no one else in the world like her," Seth agreed, seemingly reminding Auggie that he wasn't just thinking aloud.

With a serious expression, Auggie advised, "Prove it to her then."

Finally starting to understand what Auggie meant, by telling him to be a man, he asked, "Any ideas?"

"Are you coming to the wedding?"

"It's invitation only."

"Then I'd say it's about time you had a talk with your parents. Don't ya think."

Seth lifted his glass, drinking his whiskey down before nodding.

Auggie refilled both their glasses as he imparted, "There may not be a boyfriend graveyard, but just so ya know, if you hurt my sister I will stomp you ass into the ground." Seth nodded, knowing he would before Auggie lifted his glass and tipped it in Seth's direction, assuring, "Aside from that, you have my blessing."

Tipping his own glass toward Auggie, Seth knew what he needed to do.

Thirty One

Three showers, six hours, one forty-five minute nap and what felt like teetering on the overdose line with his intake of aspirin, Seth was finally starting to feel like he hadn't woken up that morning on a bar room floor. Which, he in fact did. He was still slightly queasy but that was normal since he was about to knock on his parents front door.

The door opened revealing a hard expression from his father, glaring at him as though he were a stranger.

"May I come in?"

Without any real sign of emotion, Leonard asked, "Were you invited?"

"No sir."

There was no response from his father.

The back of Seth's neck and shoulder's tensed as he stated, "I would like to have a conversation with you."

"Are you unable to make a phone call?"

Taking a step back, he explained, "I apologize."

Leonard stared at him, narrowing his eyes at first then relaxed his expression slightly.

"What exactly makes you think you are welcome here?"

It was possible that Seth's determination gave him the strength to say, "Nothing."

Instantly agreeing, Leonard stated, "That is correct. You have never lived up to the expectations of this family."

Seth drew in a long controlled breath before nodding.

"I apologize for not being the son you wanted. For constantly disappointing you, that was never my intention. I am also sorry for bringing Penny with me to the hospital benefit. That was a mistake and has forced me to take a long hard look at myself as a man."

With a suspicious expression, his father replied, "Continue."

"I made a decision concerning my future last night that I honestly wish I had made sooner."

"Are you seeking my approval?" Leonard questioned in a condescending tone.

"No sir," Seth stated before assuring, "I am striving to be the man I should have been all along."

"Exactly how do you expect anyone to believe that after the embarrassment you have caused this family?"
For the first time in his life, Seth stood up tall in front of his father.

"I don't. That's why I intend to prove it."

⌘

Certainly not expecting the workout she was getting, in heels, Penny walked back to Charlotte's tent.

The wedding was taking place outdoors on her Uncle Brennen's property. She originally thought it was an awesome idea to have an Auggie tent behind the altar and a Charlotte one on the opposite end of the aisle. Now it seemed like a giant pain. Not to mention that the couple to be was driving her crazy. First, Auggie sent her a text asking her to come to his tent but not tell Charlotte. Then once she got there, Braden had not shown up. When he finally did arrive, he refused to go inside. He just said 'Nah, I'm good' and stood off to the side, even though Auggie wanted him in there with him.

Now, she was headed back to crazy tent number two, where just seconds before Auggie called her to his tent, Charlotte had decided that the bobby pin that fell out of her hair meant Auggie was going to change his mind and bail on her at the last minute. And that was directly after a twenty minute rant insisting that weddings were invented by the devil.

It had already been a long day and it was only two o'clock. Regardless, knowing how happy everyone would be the minute the ceremony started was enough to keep a smile on her face and give her a cheery disposition. Even if every other minute it seemed like the whole thing was going to fall apart.

As soon as she stepped into Charlotte's tent Silvia rushed up to her.

"Is Braden here?"

Charlotte raised her eyebrows, also waiting for Penny's answer, like it was a make or break question for the day.

"Yes, he is. I just talked to him."

As Silvia squealed with delight, Charlotte sighed with relief.

Then with a panicked expression, Charlotte asked, "He's wearing a tux right."

Giving her an encouraging smile, Penny replied, "Yes he is. He looks nice too. All four of them do."

Charlotte looked up, barely moving her lips but it was enough for Penny to notice she was counting backwards in her head.

"It's going to be okay," Penny assured before Lola ran into the tent.

"Mom can't find it!" she blurted, sending Charlotte into another pre-wedding 'moment'.

As her chest started to heave, Charlotte tugged at the waist of her dress right below the peacock blue sash.

"That's it. It's not happening. I'm not getting married today."

Rolling her eyes and shaking her head, Penny asked, "What's wrong now?"

"I can't find my garter."

In all the craziness of the day Penny had forgotten her special wedding gift to Charlotte.

"Relax," she said with a smile.

Narrowing her eyes at Penny, Charlotte stated, "I am relaxed. I have come to terms with this."

Laughing, Penny replied, "Okay Miss Relaxed. Would you like to open a present?"

Standing still, Charlotte actually looked a little lost as she nodded.

Skipping over to her purse in the corner of the tent, Penny pulled out a square gift box. Smiling at it, she made her way back to Charlotte and handed it over.

After making quick work of the bow, Charlotte opened the box, looked inside and said, "It's perfect."

They both grew teary-eyed over the peacock feather garter that lay inside the box.

As Charlotte hugged her, Penny shared, "Wedding or not you're my sister. Please be my brother's wife today."

Charlotte held onto her tighter.

Penny was about to cry but they were going to be happy tears.

"Y'all are hugging without me?" Liv's voice rang through the tent.

Penny and Charlotte let go of each other as they turned toward her voice.

Both drew out a, "Da-amn," when they looked at her.

Making a clicking sound with her mouth as she winked and nodded at them, Liv was wearing a purple strapless satin dress that flawlessly hugged every curve and fell just above her knees. Her long black hair was pulled to one side and large soft curls fell over her left shoulder.

"Has Kieran seen you yet?" Charlotte questioned.

"Nah, he left the house before I got ready this morning."

The fact that Liv had been a tight pants and tank tops kind of girl since Penny had met her compelled her to ask, "Do you feel as gorgeous as you look?"

"Ha!" Liv blurted before sharing, "Yea, but I miss my socks."

Glancing down at the shiny black stilettos on Liv's feet, Penny assured, "Gah, you look incredible."

Liv flashed a genuine smile before saying, "We have a problem."

Penny's shoulders slouched as she thought, 'What now'.

Liv wore an apologetic expression as she took a step closer to her.

"For one, Lurker showed up with his parents."

Squeezing her eyes closed for a moment as Charlotte placed a comforting hand on her shoulder, Penny shook off the sudden surge of sadness, asking, "And two?"

"Your mom pretty much told his mom off."

"What?" Penny blurted, hearing Charlotte starting to laugh.

"It was kinda awesome actually. Sarah was all, 'Who the hell do you think you are', then his mom called her low class and Sarah said 'My daughter is perfect and too good for you people', but then..."

Hesitantly, Penny asked, "But then what?"

"His mom said, 'Working in a tattoo parlor, I think not'."

Before Penny could process what Liv had just shared, a familiar, "Penny Rosin Caffrey!" radiated through the tent. Penny froze seeing the angry expression her mom's face.

Marching straight up to her, Sarah appeared furious.

"I cannot believe you!" she fussed before looking back at Liv, blaming, "This is your doing." Before Penny could open her mouth, Sarah turned back to her, assuring, "You are quitting that job and you are moving back home."

Frustrated by the fact that it seemed like everyone was doing their best to make what was supposed to be such a happy day miserable for her, Penny had had enough.

"Mom!"

Sarah jumped a little at her outburst before snapping, "Don't you raise your voice to me."

Taking a deep breath, Penny informed, "I know you're disappointed in me. You can be mad all you want, but save it for tomorrow because your son is fixing to get married," before motioning to Charlotte saying, "See, here is his beautiful bride."

Sarah made an aggravated sound at Penny before focusing on Charlotte and complimenting, "You do look beautiful."

With a soft smile, Charlotte replied, "Thank you Mrs. Caffrey."

After returning her smile, Sarah pursed her lips at Penny, "I never said I was disappointed in you." Then leaving the tent, she glanced back, saying, "You look nice too, Liv."

Liv appeared stunned as she blurted, "What the hell? Did she just give me a compliment?"

Penny was pretty shocked as well at the way her mom backed down.

As Penny, Charlotte and Liv looked at each other in surreal amazement, Amila stepped in notifying, "Alright girls, it's time."

After another hug that was shared with Liv this time, Penny followed Amila and Liv out of Charlotte's tent just as Emerson walked in.

Outside the front of Charlotte's tent, everyone was getting situated in the right order, until Kieran caught a glimpse of Liv. Instead of stopping at Penny's side, he followed his wife. She watched Liv stop and turn, smiling brightly at him as she smoothed his tied down. They were too far away for her to hear what they were saying to each other. That was probably for the best judging by the expression on Kieran's face when he saw Liv was enough to let her know the heels and dress had done their job. Smiling to herself, although she didn't want to think about their sex life, she was happy for them.

Waiting for Kieran to make his way back, Penny felt a tap on her shoulder. Turning back, she immediately scowled at the expression on Braden's face.

"Why is she dressed like that?" he griped in a hushed tone.

"Stop it," Penny scolded in a low voice.

"That's not her."

"Her husband seems to like it," she gritted out trying to keep her voice down.

Stepping closer to Penny, Braden quietly bit out, "She's gotta change who she is for him to want her?"
Braden was a dumbass for sure, but nothing that went on was lost on him.

Pointing her finger at him, she warned, "Don't. That is between them. So just stop it, right now," in an angry whisper.
Shaking his head with an infuriated expression, Braden stepped back next to Silvia.

Once Kieran was back at her side, the music started to play, and Lola headed down the aisle with her basket of tiny white feathers that she sprinkled on her way down. Penny hooked her arm around Kieran's when it was their turn and smiled at Auggie the entire way to the altar. Purposely keeping her eyes fixed on the Caffrey side of the guests, she didn't want to see Seth and get upset. Braden still looked mad while Silvia appeared to be in heaven as she clung to him on their way down. Taking a deep breath, she smiled at

Ailin and Jenna making their way towards her, it was almost time.

Just as the wedding march started, Penny noticed Kieran take a step back. Ailin seemed to be keeping his distance also as Auggie and Braden stepped closer to each other. 'Oh my dear lord' was the only thing that ran through Penny's mind as she watched Braden give Auggie a little shove. Auggie shoved him back, slightly harder and before she knew it, they were rolling down the aisle.

Immediately looking at Reverend Gary, he appeared too mortified to be of any help. Penny looked to Kieran next, who seemed to think it was amusing, and Ailin gave her a 'Yea right' expression when she raised her eyebrows at him, suggesting he intervene. Searching for assistance through the sea of her family that sat there doing nothing, her mom was shaking her head with the same exasperated expression as she did when they were growing up. Ren had her hand over her mouth and Jackson had both his hands over his face. Not only that, those who weren't laughing appeared to be placing bets.

Deciding to take matters into her own hands, Penny started snapping her fingers and clapping her hand at them hoping to remind them where they were. It was no use. Braden was on his back and Auggie was basically sitting on him, holding Braden's wrists to the ground. They continued to struggle with each other until the music stopped and they looked up causing Penny to do the same.

With Emerson at her side, Charlotte looked down at them. Penny couldn't hear her words but saw her mouth move as Auggie instantly let go of Braden and stood up with the biggest smile she had ever seen on her brother's face. Charlotte curled the corner of her mouth into a smile as she watched Auggie reach down and help Braden to his feet. Back in their positions, they straightened their ties and dusted themselves off. If it weren't for the fact that Emerson kept clearing his throat to keep from laughing as he gave Charlotte away, it was like nothing ever happened.

⌘

Sitting with his parents, Seth was impatiently biding his time until the ceremony was over. He hadn't been able to take his eyes off of Penny since she made her way down the aisle. He was anxious, but the anxiety he felt was the best kind there was.

Before the ceremony started, when Sarah came up to him he felt like a traitor, especially since he would have loved to give her a high five for the way she let his mom have it. He ended up having to settle for catching up to her and quickly explaining why he was there on her way to no doubt fuss at Penny after finding out where she's been working.

Auggie and Braden's fight, although wildly inappropriate, somehow seemed to fit the occasion. They were definitely an interesting bunch, but all of them loved each other and knew what was really important in life. Just like the moment Auggie and Charlotte looked at each other, nothing else mattered. They were family.

As Seth watched Mr. Roberts give Charlotte away, his parents were expressing the disdain for the wedding party and all those included in the gathering, except themselves of course.

"And Ellis favors them. It is clear she should step down if he holds that type of judgment," Linda spouted.

Leonard's tone was harsh as he stated, "Deplorable."

Linda was quick to agree, saying, "Can you imagine being part of a family like that."

Without a second thought, Seth replied, "Yes."

As soon as the word left his mouth, Auggie's voice was inside his head griping, 'Prove it'. With Auggie in his head and Penny in his heart, Seth stood up.

Both his parents appeared outraged as Leonard demanded, "What exactly do you think you are doing?"
All Seth's statements during his earlier conversation with his father were true. How Leonard took them, was out of his hands.

"Becoming the man I should have been all along."
Keeping his eyes on Penny the entire way, he walked down the outside row of guests.

Penny didn't notice him at all, no one other than his parents did. Everyone was focused on Charlotte and Auggie. Until, Seth walked past Charlotte's sisters and stood in front of her.

The Reverend had just started, "Dearly Beloved we are..." before trailing off at his interruption.
Seth took one look at Penny's wide eyes and startled expression, and taking her face in his hands, kissed her full on her lips.

The second he let go, she quietly scolded, "You can't just come up and kiss me in the middle of my brother's wedding."

Biting the corner of his bottom lip, he replied, "I just did," actually proud of himself.
Before Penny he never would have been brave enough to do something like this.

"Go sit down," she fussed before questioning, "What are you thinking?"

Smiling down at her, he replied, "I'm thinking that I'm willing to make a fool of myself in front of everyone here because I love you. You're every happy moment in my life. You're my one. My one Penny." Watching her purse her lips into a smile, Seth went down on one knee, proposing, "Will you marry me?"
Her eyes grew teary as they sparkled down at him.

Standing up in front of her, Seth leaned down to kiss her again, when he heard Auggie clear his throat.

"You know, when I said you had my blessing, this isn't what I meant."

Giving Auggie his best 'Sorry but not sorry' expression, Seth watched Charlotte take Auggie's hand and kiss him on the cheek.

As Auggie turned to her and smiled, the Reverend seemed to have had enough.

Slamming his hand down on the altar, he shouted, "This is supposed to be a solemn occasion."

Everyone started to laugh, causing the Reverend's face to turn bright red.

"That's it! This is the last family wedding I'm doing!" he swore before snapping, "Auggie, you gonna marry her?"

Glaring at him, he replied, "Yes."

"Charlotte, you really want to marry into this?" the Reverend questioned.

With a smile on her face, she answered, "Yes."

"Then kiss her, your married," he griped before stomping off saying, "I need a damn drink."

"I think we broke Reverend Gary," Braden blurted, causing everyone to start laughing again.

Everything fell quiet. Auggie and Charlotte were sharing a moment with each other that made Seth smile in his happiness for them.

Sliding his hand around Penny's, Seth leaned to her ear, whispering, "Can we have cinnamon rolls for breakfast?"

Penny threw her arms around his neck in response. He was just about to kiss her when they heard Charlotte let out a yelp. Turning together, to see what happened, they watched Auggie hoisting her up and tossing her over his shoulder.

As everyone stood up and clapped and hollered and laughed, for the newlyweds, Liv reached her hand out and high-fived Charlotte as she hung over Auggie's shoulder while he carried her down the aisle.

Seth and Penny turned back to each other at the exact same time.

"I feel it's only fair to warn you, it only gets worse. My family is insane," Penny said with a smile.

Nodding, Seth smiled before sharing, "So a... Not to pressure you or anything but a... You never answered me."

Slightly shaking her head at him, she appeared confused.

With a hopeful expression, he asked, "Will you marry me?"

With a cheery smile, she replied, "Yes," before pulling him down to meet her in a kiss.

⌘

Standing next to the wooden dance floor, that was in the field next to the open party tents, with Seth's arms around her, Penny watched her brother and his new wife slow dancing. Kieran and Liv were holding hands next to her, while Braden stood on her other side.

Penny could tell something was still bothering him even though he seemed alright with Kieran and Liv now. She imagined it was just the fact that once again he was the odd man out.

"Wanna dance?" Braden offered when Silvia walked by.

Giving him a nasty expression, she blurted, "Uh, no," and kept on walking.

Penny couldn't help but laugh as he looked at her and said, "Guess she's over me."

"Awe, I'll dance with you Punk," Liv offered before Kieran pulled her back to him saying, "This one's mine."

With a surprised look on her face, she asked, "You're gonna dance with me."

"Baby, I'm gonna do all kinds of things with you," as he led her onto the floor.

Penny scrunched her face up and shook her head before Liv looked back at Braden saying, "I catch ya next go round."

Braden flashed a smile at her that quickly vanished the second she turned around.

"You okay?" Seth asked him.

Braden patted Seth on the back and winked at Penny before stepping away.

Leaning to her ear, Seth held her a little tighter.

"Would you like to dance?"

Turning her head, she met him in a soft kiss before saying, "I sure would."

Keeping one of his arms around her, he led her onto the dance floor.

Pulling her close, Seth swore, "I love you, Penny Caffrey."

"I love you too," she assured, swaying back and forth with him.

This was the happiest day of her life and she knew in her heart, with Seth, there would be many more to come.

The End

Epilogue

Penny stood outside the marking room with flutters of anticipation in her stomach.

As Kieran unlocked the door Liv patted her on the shoulder, saying, "I'll send him back when he gets here." Stepping inside, she looked around. There were pictures of each marker throughout Caffrey history, since photographs that is, hanging on the walls. In the center of the room there was what Penny thought looked like an old fashioned dentist chair with a wooden stool sitting beside it. Behind the chair was Kieran's set up next to a rectangular wooden table. Sitting on the table, sat Kieran's legacy. A log book of Celtic hearts all recorded from the beginning of the tradition.

Over the last few months, Penny's skill had improved along with her own client list at Legacy Ink. This, however, was the proudest moment of her life.

"You're the first woman to step a foot into the marking room, Pen," Kieran shared in a somber tone, closing the door behind them.

Nodding at him, she asked, "What do you think they would say?" pointing to the pictures on the wall.

Kieran's eyes noticeably focused on his father's picture before he replied, "Doesn't matter. We're here and they're not. This is our Legacy now." Teary eyed at his words and the pride she felt in her heart, Penny walked behind the chair to prepare.

It wasn't long before there a tap on the door. Excitement hummed inside of Penny as Kieran let Seth into the room.

Standing at the log book, she smiled at Seth's nervous expression, sharing, "I need your mark." Seth glanced at the chair he was about to sit in and handed her a square slip of paper.

Seeing the mark he chose, two interlocking hearts exactly like the one on her wrist, Penny started to smile then scowled questioning, "Why didn't mom add the Celtic heart?"

"She offered but I wanted her to leave the center open." Penny felt conflicted, the Celtic heat was part of the tradition. Hesitantly, she looked to Kieran for approval.

With a quick nod he imparted, "Your mark. Your call."

Seth took her wrist in his hand, placing his thumb in the center of her tattoo sharing, "That's where I can feel your heat beat. That is where mine beats too."
Pushing up on her tip-toes, she slid her hands around the back of his neck, pulling him into a kiss.

"Hey now, we don't do that in here," Kieran fussed, interrupting their moment.

Rolling her eyes, Penny let go and said, "Have a seat," before turning back to the log book.
As Seth seated himself in the chair, Penny wrote down their names and the date before watching Kieran take a gold coin in the shape of a heart with a raised Celtic knot in the center out of his pocket. He pressed it to a pad of ink next to the log book before stamping it beside their names.

Whatever bravery Seth had managed to work up seemed to vanish.

"Remind me again why your family does this," he said, watching the needle head towards his chest.

Kieran replied, "Well now, that's my favorite story to tell."
Penny gave a comforting smile as she placed her hand on the center of Seth's chest, watching him relax almost instantly under her touch.

⌘

Closing his eyes, Seth listened to the story of Kieran's legacy as Penny, his One Penny, placed her mark upon the left side of his chest.

Legacy
The Legend of Fergus & Cinnie

Celtic tattoos began as warrior markings. Intimidating the enemy going into battle. Along time ago, a Celt named Fergus marked his heart for everyone to see. Fergus was a hard core warrior and womanizer. Battles, different women, that sort of thing.

Legend has it, a neighboring clan was being invaded. Fergus, who was always up for a good fight, left without hesitation. The battle was won and the neighboring clan was so grateful for his assistance, he was offered... Well, pretty much whatever he wanted.

The idea was brought about to join the clans through Fergus and Cinnie, the neighboring clan elder's daughter. Cinnie was of course obedient to her father but not so interested in having a man like Fergus as a husband. He was rough, rude and from years of battle not the best looking. However, Fergus was instantly attracted to her. Cinnie was young and beautiful and Fergus swore the moment he saw her, his heart beat as if he were rushing into war. Cinnie would not refuse her father and the two were joined but she had no problem refusing Fergus, in the bedroom that is. He tried everything from bringing her flowers to learning to play the harp in hopes to woo her.

Years passed and not much changed, he still wooed her every day and she still refused him just the same. Until one day Fergus didn't return home. Now it's been said, he was ambushed and captured and he fought his way out and its also told that he was in a drunken stupor caused by Cinnie not returning his affections.

Regardless of the reason, for the first time since they had been wed, Cinnie spent the night alone. There was no one there to lay flowers on the table, attempt to play and sing made up songs of her beauty or even snore to keep her awake at night. The next morning, she woke to a quiet house. As she sat there praying for the rough, rude, often obnoxious and almost hideous man she had been forced to share a home with, Cinnie remembered all the things Fergus had done to gain her affection. When he wandered up the next afternoon, Cinnie flogged him something fierce, damn near knocking him unconscious. She then told him that he was never to leave her again because she loved him. After she gave him a homecoming that would put any honeymoon to shame, he went down and had a knotted heart marked on the left side of his chest. When the man marking him asked why, he said it was because the greatest battle he ever fought was the one for her heart.

Hagen Caffrey was so moved by Fergus' sentiment he wrote the story down and when his oldest son found the one he was meant to spend the rest of his life with, he told him the story and marked his heart. Creating a legacy that has been handed down from father to son along with the trade.

Playlist

Music has a way of inspiring the smallest ideas. It allows me to create an entire scene or chapter from just the right song. For me, music is one of the most important creative tools there is. These are the songs that brought One Penny to life.

The Lazy Song-Bruno Mars
Got You-The Flys
Not Your Fault-Awolnation
Riptide-Vance Joy
Shake It Off-Taylor Swift
Sleeping With A Friend-Neon Trees
Stolen Dance-Milky Chance
Walking On Sunshine-Katrina & The Waves
Brass Monkey-The Beastie Boys

About the Author

M. Sembera was born in Baton Rouge, Louisiana and now lives in Brazoria, Texas with her husband, three kids, three dogs and two cats. After writing her first short story when she was in high school, M. instantly fell in love with writing. However, life sometimes gets in the way of aspirations and it wasn't until years later, when her life calmed down, M. was able to start writing again.

'For me, each new book I write or character I create feels like the first time and I find myself falling in love with writing all over again'

Past works include Charlotte, Enduring Everything, 'The Rennillia Series'.

www.BrokenBirdMedia.com

Up Next

Marked Heart